WONDER PETS!

JOIN THE CIRCUS

adapted by Josh Selig and Melanie Pal
illustrated by Alexandria Fogerty, Little Airplane Productions

SIMON SPOTLIGHT/NICKELODEON

New York   London   Toronto   Sydney

SIMON SPOTLIGHT

An imprint of Simon & Schuster Children's Publishing Division
1230 Avenue of the Americas, New York, New York 10020
© 2008 Viacom International Inc. All rights reserved. NICK JR., *Wonder Pets!*, and all related titles, logos, and characters
are trademarks of Viacom International Inc.
All rights reserved, including the right of reproduction in whole or in part in any form.
SIMON SPOTLIGHT and colophon are registered trademarks of Simon & Schuster, Inc.
Manufactured in the United States of America
First Edition
10 9 8 7 6 5 4 3 2 1
ISBN-13: 978-1-4169-7581-6
ISBN-10: 1-4169-7581-0

It was the last day of school before break, and all the kids were heading out the door. Linny the Guinea Pig, Turtle Tuck, and Ming-Ming Duckling were sitting patiently in their cages.

"The kids are on vacation and won't be coming to school for a while," explained Linny.

"What will we do while the kids are away?" wondered Ming-Ming.

Just then the Wonder Pets heard a rumbling noise. They ran to the window and saw a colorful train passing by.

"Ooh, a pretty train!" said Tuck.

"Full of animals!" said Ming-Ming.

"Wonder Pets!" said Linny. "That's not just any train. That's a circus train!"

"Let's build a special Flyboat and fly over there," suggested Linny.
"That way we can see the animals up close."
The Wonder Pets sang as they built their Circus Boat:

Linny, Tuck, and Ming-Ming hopped in their Circus Boat and took off for the circus train.

"This is the greatest Circus Boat on Earth!" shouted Ming-Ming.

The Wonder Pets swooped down beside the train to get a better view. In the windows they saw lots of different animals, all practicing their circus routines—and the penguin ringmaster, too!

The Wonder Pets noticed a little lion cub walking on top of the last car.
Suddenly the train jolted, and the little lion cub slipped to the edge.

"The lion cub!" yelled Tuck. "He's going to fall!"

"This is serious!" said Ming-Ming.

Linny, Tuck, and Ming-Ming knew they had to save the little lion cub!
"Let's hold hands and make a chain!" said Linny.
"Then we can swing the lion cub into the Circus Boat!" said Tuck.

Using teamwork, the Wonder Pets got the little lion cub into the Circus Boat!

"My name is Cubby," the lion cub said. "Thanks for saving me, Wonder Pets!"

"You're welcome, little cub-a-roo!" said Tuck.

"Saving little animals is just what we do!" Ming-Ming chimed in.

The penguin ringmaster thought the Wonder Pets were so special that he asked them to join his circus!

The Wonder Pets followed the train to the circus tent. As they flew, they sang:

Wonder Pets! Wonder Pets!
We're on our way!
To join the circus
on our holiday!

We're not too tough!
And we're not too big!
But somehow we got a circus gig!

Goooooo, Wonder Pets! Yay!

When they arrived at the circus tent, Cubby, Baby Panda, and Baby Monkey showed the Wonder Pets around. What a sight to see!

It was time for the big show! Linny, Tuck, and Ming-Ming took their places in the circus rings. Linny was spinning plates on stalks of celery.

Tuck was a clown doing lots of silly things to make the audience laugh.
Ming-Ming was twirling gracefully on a silk ribbon high in the air.

Cubby, Baby Panda, and Baby Monkey couldn't wait to see the show! The three little animals climbed to the very top of the high-wire platform to get a better view. But it wasn't a safe place to be!

Oh, no! Just as the Wonder Pets were finishing their acts, the baby animals slipped from the platform! They were dangling high above the stage, holding on to a thin rope.

"Help! Help!" cried the baby animals.

The Wonder Pets looked up from the stage and saw the three baby animals in trouble. They began to sing:

Linny! Tuck! And Ming-Ming, too!
We're Wonder Pets and we'll help you!

The Wonder Pets sprang into action and raced to the top of the trapeze.

Linny remembered how they saved
Cubby when he was slipping off the train.
The Wonder Pets held hands and made a chain!
"Come on, Wonder Pets! Let's swing the
baby animals to safety!" encouraged Linny.

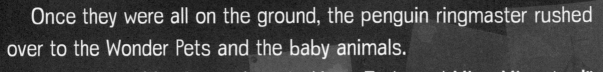

Once they were all on the ground, the penguin ringmaster rushed over to the Wonder Pets and the baby animals.

"Let's give a big circus cheer to Linny, Tuck, and Ming-Ming, too!" said the penguin ringmaster.

"Hip, hip, hooray!" cheered all the animals.

Then everyone celebrated with some celery!

"You should perform that teamwork act every night!" said the penguin ringmaster.

"Thanks, Mr. Penguin ringmaster boss, sir," said Ming-Ming.

"But we'd rather go back to the classroom and keep saving baby animals," Tuck said.

"You can hire Cubby, Baby Panda, and Baby Monkey for your circus!" suggested Linny.

"That's a great idea!" said the penguin ringmaster. "I've got a good feeling about these critters!"

The Wonder Pets hurried back to the schoolhouse. As they got closer, Tuck and Ming-Ming began to talk excitedly.

"Ah, home sweet home!" said Tuck. "I love my tank."

"And I love my swing!" added Ming-Ming.

Linny smiled. The Wonder Pets would never forget their amazing circus adventure, but it was good to be home.

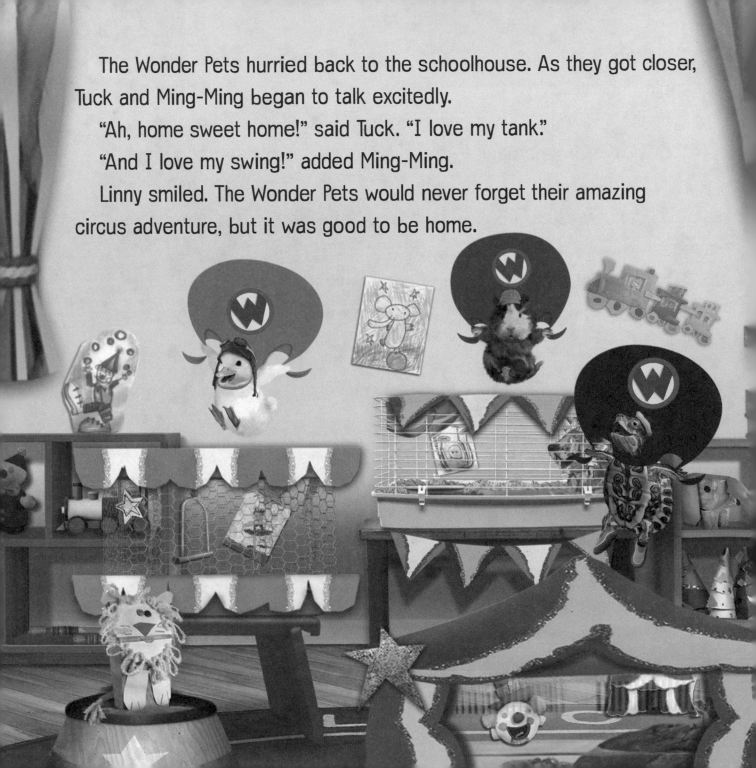

THE PRINCETON REVIEW

PAYING FOR GRADUATE SCHOOL

WITHOUT GOING BROKE

Random House, Inc., New York
www.PrincetonReview.com

2005 Edition

Princeton Review Publishing, L.L.C.
2315 Broadway
New York, NY   10024
E-mail: bookeditor@review.com

ISBN: 0-375-76422-4

Editor: Erik Olson
Production Editor: Vivian Gomez
Production Coordinator: Scott Harris

Manufactured in the United States of America on partially recycled paper.

9 8 7 6 5 4 3 2 1

2005 Edition

ACKNOWLEDGMENTS

Both authors wish to acknowledge the patience and skillful word processing of Janine Meersman, who labored many hours over many revisions of various drafts of the manuscript.

CONTENTS

So You Want to Go to Graduate School

Why Do You Want to Go to Graduate School?

High school trained you to be a functional citizen in society. College exposed you to the breadth and depth of human achievement and potential. But it is graduate school that prepares you for a *profession*. Whether you are considering a master's degree in occupational therapy or a PhD in art history, your course of study will focus on providing you with the information necessary to begin a *career*. You will be learning material not just to pass the next test but to use for the rest of your professional life. Therefore, if the subject matter doesn't interest you, or if the job options upon graduation don't appear to be that rewarding—either financially or professionally—put down this book and reevaluate your decision to apply. Graduate school is strenuous, time-consuming, and expensive—sometimes not only for you, but for your loved ones as well. However, you and your peers will be working at the edge of intellectual discovery. The idea of being a member of that academic vanguard, then, is the key to success in graduate school.

Types of Degrees

Graduate programs can be divided into professional and research degrees. **Professional degrees** include medical, law, nursing, and dental degrees, as well as master's degrees in business administration, divinity, and allied health. A more extensive list appears on page 6.

Professional Degrees

This is a small sample of professional degrees. What they all have in common is that they are largely course credit–based and do not require a significant research project. Many master's programs are offered via distance learning as well as in person.

Allied Health

Advanced Nursing Degrees	MSN
Audiology	MS
Community Health	MS
Medical Technician	MS
Occupational Therapy	MS
Physical Therapy	MS
Public Health/Epidemiology	MPH, DPH
Speech Pathology	MCH
Architecture	MArch
Business	MBA
Dental	DDS
Divinity	MDiv
Education	MEd, EdD
Engineering	MEng, DEng
Forestry	MF
Journalism	MJ
Landscape Architecture	MLA
Law	JD
Library	MLS
Medicine	MD, DO
Music Performance	MM
Public Policy	MPP
Social Work	MSW
Urban Design	MUD
Veterinary Medicine	DVM
Optometry	OD

Professional degrees are generally course-intensive and time-limited. In other words, you take classes and graduate with the same cohort of classmates, usually over a specified period of time. The purpose of your education is to teach you the knowledge and skills necessary to practice a certain profession, such as medicine or law. This educational process superficially resembles an extension of the undergraduate academic experience, but the course material is more specialized and pitched at a much higher level. Furthermore, the application process has also selected an entire class of bright individuals with a common goal. The professional degree also differs from the undergraduate degree in that it often involves cooperatives, internships, group projects, and other types of experiential learning. Finally, many careers require not only the professional degree, but also a certification examination administered by an accreditation agency. For example, to become a doctor in the United States, you must pass the United States Medical Licensing Examination (USMLE), sponsored by the Federation of State Medical Boards of the United States and the National Board of Medical Examiners. Upon graduation and certification, your desirability in the job market will depend on your class standing and the academic reputation of your department and university.

Funding for professional school is limited and therefore competitive. Still, there are fellowship and federal aid opportunities to help cover the cost of a professional education (see part 3), and the sizable salary that you will command with most professional degrees will allow for a quick and relatively painless repayment of educational loans.

Research degrees include both the master's and the doctorate. You can, for example, obtain a Master of Arts in history, a Master of Fine Arts in creative writing, or a PhD in electrical engineering.

Master of Fine Arts (MFA)
These programs involve both course work and a creative project. Often many of the individual disciplines are housed in an art, performing arts, or (in the case of creative writing) English department.
Art
Art Education
Art History (also MA, PhD)
Art Therapy
Ceramics
Creative Writing
Dance
Drawing
Electronic Integrated Arts
Film and Video
Glass
Graphic Design
Historic Preservation
Interior Design
Jewelry Design
Metalsmithing
Painting
Photography
Printmaking
Sculpture
Studio and Applied Art
Textile Design/Fibers
Theatre/Performing Arts

The Master of Arts or Master of Science generally takes two years of full-time study. These degrees are course-intensive and include a departmental comprehensive examination and a small-scale research project or other original piece of work. This project is accomplished with the critical assistance of a faculty advisor. Financial aid, in the form of tuition scholarships and stipends, is more likely in science and engineering and in departments whose terminal degree—the highest degree attainable—is a master's. In other words, you are more likely to find institutional funding (money from the college) at Smith College, where the highest biology degree is a master's, than at the University of Massachusetts—only 10 miles away—where the terminal degree in biology is a PhD. For a master's degree, the recommendation of your graduate advisor, the academic reputation of your department and university, and your demonstrated job skills will play a larger role in getting a job than the outcome of your research project.

The Master of Fine Arts (MFA) is a terminal degree. That means the MFA is the highest degree that an artist can earn in his or her field. Funding, however, is not much better than for master's programs in the humanities. One way in which the MFA differs greatly from the MA is in what you need to bring to the job market. Your portfolio of work is a more important credential than a master's thesis.

Research Degrees		
Some MA, MS, and all PhD degrees are awarded as research degrees. Many disciplines may be housed in a large department; for instance, a biology department may have faculty working in several of the life science disciplines.		
	# of Graduate Programs	**Annual # of PhDs (00–02)**
LIFE SCIENCES		
Animal Science		363
Aquaculture and Fisheries, Domestic Animal Sciences, Wildlife Science		
Biochemistry, Biophysics, and Structural Biology	227	920
Biochemistry, Biophysics, Structural Biology		
Cell Biology	217	344
Developmental Biology	159	302
Ecology and Evolutionary Biology	159	302
Behavior and Ethology, Biogeochemistry, Evolution, Population Biology, Physiological Ecology, Terrestrial and Aquatic Ecology		
Entomology		113
Food Science and Engineering		146
Food Engineering and Processing, Food Microbiology, Food Chemistry, Food Biotechnology		
Genetics, Genomics, and Bioinformatics	110	213
Bioinformatics, Genetics, Genomics		
Immunology and Infectious Disease		261
Immunity, Immunology of Infections Disease, Immunopathology, Immunoprophylaxis and Therapy Parasitology		
Microbiology		402
Environmental Micro and Ecology, Microbial Physiology, Pathogenic Microbiology, Virology		
Molecular Biology		709
Neuroscience Neurobiology	154	469
Cognitive Neuroscience, Computational Neuroscience, Molecular and Cellular Neuroscience, Systems Neuroscience		
Nutrition		129
Animal, Human, Community, and International Nutrition		
Pharmacology, Toxicology, and Environmental Health	164	442
Environmental Health, Pharmacology, Toxicology, Medicinal/Pharmaceutical Chemistry		
Physiology and Anatomy	176	233
Plant Sciences		593
Agronomy, Horticulture and Crop Sciences, Forestry and Forest Sciences, Horticulture, Plant Pathology, Plant Breeding and Genetics		
Emerging Fields		
Biotechnology, Systems Biology		

	# of Graduate Programs	Annual # of PhDs (00–02)
HUMANITIES		
American Studies		113
Classics	47	65
Classical Literature Philology, Ancient History, Ancient Philosophy, Classical Archaelogy and Art History, Indo-European Linguistics and Philology		
Comparative Literature	71	186
English Language and Literature	146	1,023
American Literature; Cultural Studies; English Literature until 1800; English Literature after 1800; Ethnic and Minority American Literature; Feminist, Gender, and Sexuality Studies; Theory		
French and Francophone Language and Literature	79	144
French Linguistics, French and Francophone Literature		
German Language and Literature	59	86
German Literature, German Linguistics		
Global Cultural Studies		96
African Studies, Asian Studies, Latin American Studies, Near Eastern Studies, Slavic Studies		
History	158	1,031
African, Asian, European, Intellectual, Latin American , Middle Eastern, United States		
History of Art, Architecture, and Archeology	58	213
American Art; Ancient, Medieval, Renaissance, Baroque; Asian; Modern; Theory and Criticism		
Music (except Performance)	89	766
Ethnomusicology, Composition, Musicology		
Philosophy	110	389
Epistemology, Ethics and Political Philosophy, History of Philosophy, Metaphysics, Philosophy of Science, Philosophy of the Mind and Language		
Religion	72	342
Spanish and Portuguese Language and Literature	84	217
Latin American Literature, Portuguese Literature, Spanish Linguistics, Spanish Literature		
Theater and Peformance Studies		95
History of Drama, Performance Studies, Theory		
Emerging Fields		
Film Studies; Feminist, Gender, and Sexuality Studies; Race, Ethnicity, and Post-colonial Studies		

	# of Graduate Programs	Annual # of PhDs (00–02)
PHYSICAL SCIENCES AND MATHEMATICS		
Applied Mathematics		235
Astrophysics and Astronomy	76	177
Chemistry	203	2,033
Computer Sciences	156	861
Artificial Intelligence, Programming Languages, Systems, Theory		
Earth Sciences	127	371
Environmental Science, Geology, Geochemistry, Geophysics and Seismology, Paleontology, Soil Science		
Mathematics	169	608
Algebra, Number Theory, Algebraic Geometry, Analysis, Discrete Mathematics and Combinatories, Geometry, Logic, Topology		
Oceanography and Atmospheric Sciences	50	309
Atmospheric Sciences, Fresh Water Studies, Meteorology, Oceanography		
Physics	182	1,223
Atomic; Molecular; and Optical; Condensed Matter; Cosmology; Relativity; and Gravity; Elementary Particles, Fields, and String Theory; Engineering Physics; Fluids; Nuclear; Plasma; Quantum		
Statistics and Probability	122	275
Biostatistics, Probability, Statistical Theory		
Emerging Field		
Nanoscience		

	# of Graduate Programs	Annual # of PhDs (00–02)
ENGINEERING		
Aerospace Engineering	56	208
Biological and Agricultural Engineering		
Agricultural, Bioinstrumentation, and Measurement		
Bioengineering and Biomedical Engineering	86	243
Biomechanics, Biomolecular Engineering		
Chemical Engineering	121	609
Civil and Environmental Engineering	130	577
Environmental, Environmental Fluid Mechanics and Hydrology, Environmental Systems, Geotechnical, Remote Sensing, Structural, Transportation Systems, Water Resources		
Electrical Engineering	154	1,532
Computer, Communications, Electrical and Electronics		
Materials Science and Engineering	97	416
Biological, Environmental, Devices, Structural		
Mechanical Engineering	143	890
Operations Research, Systems and Industrial Engineering	69	296
Industrial, Operational Research, Systems		
Emerging Fields		
Information Science, Nanoscience and Nanotechnology		

	# of Graduate Programs	Annual # of PhDs (00–02)
SOCIAL AND BEHAVIORAL SCIENCES		
Agricultural and Resource Economics		
Anthropolgy	95	473
Archeology, Biological and Physical, Social and Cultural		
Communications		526
Communications Studies, Mass Communication, Speech and Rhetoric		
Economics	135	1,085
Behavioral, Econometrics, Theory, Growth and Development, Industrial Organization, International, Labor, Public		
Geography and Regional Science	53	176
Linguistics	77	236
Applied; Comparative and Historical; Computational; Psycholinguistics; Sociolinguistics; Semantics, Syntax, Phonology		
Political Science	129	756
American, Comparative, International, Models and Methods, Theory, Public Policy		
Psychology	228	3,575
Biological, Clinical and Abnormal, Cognitive, Developmental, Industrial and Organizational, Social		
Sociology	125	634
Criminology, Historical, Methods and Mathematical, Social Stratification		
Emerging Fields		
Organizations, Occupations, and Work; Science and Technology Studies		

The selection of disciplines and sub disciplines is from Assessing Research-Doctorate Programs(2003),
National Academies Press, Washington, DC.
The number of Graduate Programs that graduated PhDs between 1986 and 1992 is from Research Doctorate Programs
in the United States (1995). National Academies Press, Washington, DC.
The average annual output of PhDs between 2000 and 2002 is from Doctorate Recipients from
United States Universities: Summary Report (2003)

The doctorate is primarily a research degree. There may be preliminary examinations at the start of your program to determine which courses you should take, and there most certainly will be comprehensive examinations three or four years later to determine how much you know about your discipline. The time it takes for you to earn the degree, however, will largely depend on how long it takes you to develop an original idea, research it, write a dissertation, and defend your results to a faculty committee. Learning how to develop ideas, do research, and present your work involves a one-on-one relationship with a faculty mentor akin to the way medieval guilds worked. Faculty advisors not only teach you the necessary skills to do research, but are also the first to judge the originality, rigor, and importance of your final project. For the MFA, the project is most often a piece or series of pieces of original art; for advanced research degrees, it is a written master's thesis or PhD dissertation. The time it takes to finish this final project will depend on your own sense of commitment and a little bit of luck, as well as faculty expectations and support. Often it takes about six years of full-time study from the completion of your baccalaureate degree to the time you receive your doctorate. Most full-time doctoral students are supported with tuition scholarships and/or stipends; the amount of financial aid is dependent upon the discipline and the department's funding.

After earning a doctorate, you are eligible for research positions in government, industry, and academia. Teaching and academic administrative positions are also within your purview. Your ability to compete for academic placement will depend upon your teaching experience and research potential, as demonstrated in your curriculum vitae and letters of recommendation. The academic reputations of your advisor and of the department are also factors. For nonacademic positions, relevant research skills, such as a command of statistics, Arabic, or polymerase chain reactions, are important. You must also show that you can work well in a team setting.

You may not be interested in learning how to do research or receive training for a specific profession. Maybe you are interested in focused learning in a particular technique to improve your credentials and enhance your potential at work. Maybe you really don't want to have to undergo the rigors of the admissions process, especially if you sense rejection. If either of these scenarios applies to you, you should look not only at credential programs offered through institutions of higher education, but also at programs offered through industrial centers of learning.

What If Your Interests Have Changed Since College?

Chances are they have. But you don't have to be pre-med or pre-law to get into medical or law school. You *do*, however, have to take the undergraduate courses that are prerequisites for these programs. If you're still in college, find out what the requirements are for the program you want to enter and take the courses while still an undergrad. If you've already graduated, you can take courses part-time; for some professional schools, like medicine, you can even enroll in a full-time post-baccalaureate program designed specifically to help you fulfill these requirements. Some professional master's programs actually *encourage* a different major. For example, physics majors are welcomed with open arms into science education graduate programs. Even for research degrees, only a little more than half of graduate students study the same subject as their college major. However, many disciplines, especially in science and engineering, require a considerable breadth of knowledge in the field before specializing in a subdiscipline. Even a switch from one department to another while at college—from physics to biology, for example—may affect your eligibility for certain programs. Completion of survey (introductory) courses will not be enough. If you're someone who switched majors late in college, an alternative route to your graduate program of choice could involve concentrating your efforts on a few upper-level courses related to your research interest, doing well on the specialty GRE test, and applying for a master's degree within a second-tier graduate program in order to develop the credentials necessary to get into a top PhD program.

Who Is the Typical Graduate Student?

You may be wondering what your peers will be like in your chosen discipline. Fortunately, the National Center for Educational Statistics (NCES) of the Department of Education (http://nces.ed.gov/pubsearch) and the annual *Survey of Earned Doctorates*, compiled by the University of Chicago's National Opinion Research Center (www.norc.uchicago.edu/issues/docdata.htm), attempt to answer this question.

Degrees Being Sought by Graduate Students in 1999–2000					
	MA/MS/MFA	**PhD**	**MBA**	**MEd/EdD**	**Law/Health Prof. Degree**
Age	33	34	32	38	28
Female	57%	50%	40%	73%	45%
U.S. citizen	84%	76%	85%	96%	93%
Married	56%	55%	57%	70%	25%
With dependents	27%	25%	37%	49%	19%
African American	8%	6%	15%	14%	6%
Asian American	15%	19%	19%	7%	14%
Native American	1%	1%	0.4%	0.6%	1%
Hispanic or Latino	7%	5%	8%	8%	5%
Going to a public university	55%	63%	43%	64%	41%
Full-time student	54%	69%	27%	27%	90%
Started right after BA/BS	26%	25%	12%	14%	42%
Waited >7 years after BA/BS	25%	35%	31%	33%	12%

Data from NCES study on student financing of graduate and first professional education

The data show that the typical student pursuing a law or medical degree is more likely to be younger, single, and devoting full attention to the degree. Furthermore, the law or medical student is less likely to have a campus job (or the time for one). The typical master's student, on the other hand, is older and more likely to be married. Students working on their doctorates are also older, but they are more likely to be working full-time on their studies. However, the data also show that there are significant percentages of students who don't fit this type. So another way to look at it is that no matter who you are or what you have been through, there are other students who share your experience.

Another way to look at the typical graduate student is to analyze the profile of doctorate recipients. The National Science Foundation (NSF) has broken this demographic into disciplines to provide a more granular breakdown. Each of the fields produced between 5,500 and 8,300 PhDs in 2001.

Profile of Persons Who Earned a PhD in 2001

	Education	Engineering	Social Sciences	Humanities	Physical Science	Life Sciences
Age	44	31	33	35	31	32
Female	65%	17%	54%	51%	25%	47%
U.S. citizen	84%	39%	74%	78%	52%	65%
Years enrolled in grad school	8.3	6.7	7.6	9.0	6.7	7.0
BA/BS in the same field as the PhD	33%	75%	58%	55%	64%	47%

Data from the NSF Survey of Earned Doctorates

The average person who earned a doctorate in education is different from the rest. He or she is more likely to have majored in a different field and started graduate school after working for more than 10 years. Engineers are more likely to be foreign-born males who were educated as engineers in college. More women go into the life sciences than into the physical sciences and engineering.

Take some time to study this table. Depending on your intended course of study, it can reveal to you the sort of people with whom you will probably spend most of your time for the next several years. If you don't fit the type, be prepared to be in the minority.

How to Get In

You probably chose your college for several reasons, including its academic reputation, major offerings, personal fit, cost, and location. Your choice of a graduate program will probably be based on these same considerations, only this time you know what your discipline is, you have a pretty good idea of what career path(s) might interest you, and the choice of whether and where to go is solely up to you.

Full-time or Part-time

There are several good reasons for choosing to attend graduate school full-time.

1. Time. Obviously, by attending full-time, you'll reduce the overall amount of time you spend earning your degree. Intellectual connections are better formed and strengthened when you concentrate your studies. Furthermore, your attention is less likely to wander, and you will remain focused on the goal of getting the degree.

2. Options. Full-time study also increases the number of graduate programs in which you can enroll. If you have to keep your job in order to go to school, you will be restricted to schools within close proximity. Moreover, individual professional programs, such as medical school and most doctoral research programs, simply do not accept part-time students.

3. Educational Quality. Going to school full-time fully immerses you in the academic community. You'll have more time and opportunities to interact with faculty and students in your discipline, and the network that you build is critical for your future career. The campus is a vibrant intellectual and cultural center of activity. You will be exposed to people, ideas, and activities that extend beyond your discipline. Perhaps it will be a chance to re-experience the intellectual enthusiasm of your undergraduate years with a much more mature attitude.

4. Financing. Fear of the loss of job income is probably the most frequently cited reason why students opt to go to graduate school part-time. The types and amount of university support, however, increase with full-time study. Tuition scholarships, student loans, fellowships, and stipends are often reserved for full-time students. Additional perks, such as student housing, health care, medical insurance, and day care may also be available only to full-time students. Before you reject the idea of full-time student status, you should complete Worksheet A on page 165 to determine if it is the more economical way for you to go to school. Of course, if you like your current job, you want an advanced degree to obtain a higher position with the same employer, or your employer will cover some of your educational expenses, these are good reasons for attending part-time.

A WORD ON DISTANCE EDUCATION

You may want to study for a degree the traditional way—by taking classes offered on campus—or via the Internet. Distance education has largely replaced the correspondence courses of yesteryear. Internet courses afford more communication between instructor and student via email and even among classmates in a chat room, but they suffer from a lack of personal interaction and the collegiate atmosphere. Students and faculty also can't network as easily.

Many, but not all, universities offer distance education courses and degrees. (See http://distance.gradschools.com for a consortium of physical and virtual universities.) A few, such as Capella University (www.capellauniversity.edu), the University of Phoenix (www.phoenix.edu), and Walden University (www.waldenu.edu), exist almost entirely on the Internet. Our position on distance education programs is that they work best for course-intensive, research-light certifications and professional master's degrees.

Choosing the Best Program for You

No matter what your limitations, you will want to enroll in the graduate program that has the strongest reputation and is the most affordable. Future employers *will* care where and under whom you studied. You will therefore have to carefully investigate departments that interest you. You should use several sources to inform your decision: academic advisors, program directories, individual departmental brochures and websites, national rankings of graduate programs, and, most importantly, your own opinion. Use all of them, but start with you.

First, determine which specialty or subdiscipline within a field interests you the most. For example, if you're interested in diagnosing hearing disorders, you will seek an advanced degree in audiology. Research degrees require a focus *before* choosing a program because your research interests will determine your compatibility with a program or vice versa. (For professional degrees, you won't decide upon a specialty until you're well into your program of study.) The more specific you can be in defining the focus of your research, the more likely you will be happy with your program.

You can define your direction better after brainstorming with other students who are majoring in your discipline, with professionals who are already working in the field, and especially with faculty mentors. A faculty mentor does not have to be the person who was randomly assigned to you by your college and whose duty it was to sign your semester course schedule. Choose a couple of faculty members who work in a discipline that interests you, get appointments, and knock on their doors with a list of questions. These should include:

- What sort of research in the field is hot these days?

- Who is active in this research, and where do they teach?

- What have they published recently? (You should pay special attention to this.)

- Is there any other research I should be paying attention to?

- Where is this research published?

- What kinds of jobs are available upon graduation?

- What are the positives and negatives for each field?

- Why did you get into the field?

- Given my credentials and interests, where do you think I should apply?

Then find out who else in the department specializes in the field and talk to them, too.

Only the most jaded faculty member will not respond favorably to your initiative and enthusiasm. Be prepared, however, to answer a few questions yourself:

- What are your long-term career goals? Why?

- What restrictions do you have in applying to graduate school? Do you have to go part-time and keep your full-time job? Do you have geographical restrictions?

- What courses in college didn't you like?

- How are your writing and speaking skills?

If the two of you hit it off, remember this professor when you're looking for people to write you letters of recommendation.

Staying on professors' radars is important. If you're not going to grad school right after college, make sure to find ways to stay in touch. Send Christmas or Hanukkah cards, or drop them an email once in a while.

After interrogating your new professor friends, you need to hit the campus library to continue this important research project. Search periodicals for recent articles concerning your field of interest. This will identify the major players and give you an in-depth look at recent discoveries. Note specific authors. You may not understand everything in the articles or the books you read on the subject, but the question and discussion sections should hold your interest. (If you find these dull, chances are you'll be bored studying the subject in grad school.) A recent article will also reveal where the author works and how his or her research was funded.

Once you've narrowed your choice of subdiscipline, it's time to research the programs. There are three sources: reference websites, print publications (see page 193), and local information provided by the graduate department at your college. These websites—www.PrincetonReview.com, among others—and reference books describe individual programs and may provide information on minimum standards for acceptance, graduate student financial aid, and full-time enrollment; faculty size and research interests; the average time it takes to complete a degree; and so on. With these sources, you should be able to answer most of the following questions:

1. Is a tenure-track faculty member doing the research that interests you? Emeritus faculty, lecturers, concurrent faculty, and visiting professors don't count; they cannot be your mentors.

2. Is the GRE general and/or special subject test required, and is there a minimal score necessary for admission?

3. Is there a minimum acceptable undergraduate GPA? Do post-baccalaureate work experience and high GRE scores mitigate a poor undergraduate record?

4. What is the application deadline? Can you apply electronically?

5. Does the program have prerequisite courses, majors, or advanced degrees (e.g., is a master's degree necessary for acceptance to the PhD program)?

6. What is the average enrolled time-to-degree in the department? This is useful for planning purposes.

7. Where have recent graduates gotten jobs?

8. What kinds of financial aid packages are typically offered to incoming students (i.e., stipends and tuition scholarships, or loans and work-study)? How long is this support provided? What are typical student expenses (i.e., tuition, student fees, cost of living in the area, research costs borne by the student)?

9. Whom do you contact with questions or requests?

If the school's website and brochures do not answer all the questions, call the department in which you're interested and ask the departmental secretary. She may forward you to the director of graduate studies, whose contact information you should keep close at hand.

If you have discovered faculty members with whom you might like to work, write them a letter, and follow up with an email. Express your interest in seeking their mentorship, and ask if they will have time and space to accommodate you as an advisee.

Don't be discouraged if the answer is a qualified "maybe." There's no doubt that faculty members will want more information or acceptance of your application by the graduate admissions committee before making any commitments. They may also have personal reasons for not agreeing to mentor you. Be prepared to accept them.

If you have to maintain full-time employment, your choice of schools will be geographically limited. However, if you live in school-rich surroundings, such as large urban centers or New England, you will probably have more than one school from which to choose.

If you want an advanced degree in a field that offers little financial support and a modest salary upon graduation, your choice may be restricted to public universities in your state. If your home state's institutions don't offer graduate programs in the subject that interests you, consider moving (seriously) to establish residency in a state whose universities do. Residency can be achieved relatively quickly; it usually requires only a local home address, a driver's license, and maybe a voter registration card, a paycheck stub, some utility bills from your new home address, and/or a state income tax bill. To qualify for in-state tuition and other benefits, however, you have to establish residency *before* you apply to graduate or professional school. For more strategies specific to your situation, read *How to Cut Tuition: The Complete Guide to In-State Tuition* by Daryl Todd (Atlantic Educational Publishing, 1998).

You should use your limitations to narrow your list of possible programs to less than ten. Once you've done so, check the rankings (see page 194). The National Research Council (NRC) surveyed graduate programs in the early 1980s and again in the early 1990s in order to rank them. You can find the most recent survey at the library (*Research-Doctorate Programs in the United States: Continuity and Change,* National Academy Press, 1995). The last survey included data from 1988 to 1992, and the study is due for an update in 2005. Most rankings are at the departmental level (e.g., English literature, history), except for biology, which is sorted into disciplines (e.g., genetics, cellular and developmental biology, physiology, neuroscience).

The magazine *U.S. News & World Report* publishes rankings of graduate programs once a year but surveys schools only every five years or so. Unlike the NRC survey, *U.S. News* even ranks many fields at the subdisciplinary level (e.g., it breaks down the history field into American history, European history, etc.). It also ranks biology departments as a single entity, something the NRC survey did not do in 1995. The rankings are published as part of the magazine, in a separate book, and online (www.usnews.com). Don't confuse the rankings with the annual college rankings. The undergraduate rankings are based on the general academic reputation of the entire institution, along with many other institutionally reported criteria.

The graduate rankings should not dictate where you choose to apply, but they do provide useful information. First, there is a direct correlation between ranking and selectivity. Second, it will be more difficult to gain entry into top-ranked programs. Furthermore, departmental rankings eliminate the "halo effect" that certain university names confer. (In other words, even Yale has a poor graduate program.) Third, the probability of finding a top scholar who is conducting revolutionary research increases as you go up the rankings.

None of the rankings includes every university or every field of study. In addition, rankings tend to ignore individual or emerging faculty stars who work among less-than-stellar peers. Nevertheless, committees searching to fill a research or university position will care where you were trained, and the rankings give you a good idea of what the committees will think of your program.

Finally, your list of graduate programs should be realistic. Determine if your undergraduate record, your professional or research interests, and your GRE scores make you competitive for the possible graduate programs on your list. If you aren't sure, talk to a faculty advisor or, better yet, to the director of graduate studies for the program. Pick one or two programs that might be at the optimistic end of reality, one or two that you feel confident about, and, depending on how desperate you are to get that advanced degree, a safety program.

The Graduate Record Examination (GRE)

PREPARATION

The general and subject tests cost more than $100 each, so you want to take them once, score well, and forget about them. Significant and concentrated preparation will help you do this. If you have a mediocre undergraduate grade point average or have been out of school for a while, you'll need a higher score on the GRE. If you are trying to get into a graduate program in a different discipline than the one in which you earned your bachelor's, you will have to score well in the specialty exam, if it is available. If you are a senior, do not assume that successfully completing three years of college work is preparation enough. If you have a subject exam, prepare for it *after* you take the general test.

The best GRE prep? Well, we are a bit biased, but we're confident that The Princeton Review GRE courses are the best available. We offer live and online courses that former students swear by, and our books on the general test and biology, chemistry, literature, math, and psychology subject tests are all available at your friendly neighborhood book superstore. But even if you choose not to prep with The Princeton Review, you should prep with someone for this test. It carries too much weight for you to just wing it.

Educational Testing Service (ETS), the company that develops the GRE, will send you free preparation software when you register for the test. It may take up to a month to arrive. You can also download a practice test from the GRE website (www.gre.org/pracmats.html). Since the best preparation for any standardized test is familiarity with its format and content, you should take as many practice tests as possible.

Ideally, if you're still in college, you would study for the examination over the summer between your junior and senior years and take the test before going back to school. If you're currently employed full-time, pick a month between crunch times at work. Once you set your study schedule, register for the test. A looming deadline should goad you to study regularly. The general test is most often a computer-based exam given by appointment at various testing centers, which you can find at www.gre.org/cbttest.html or by calling 800-473-2255. The subject tests, given in eight disciplines, are paper-based and are offered only three times a year (April, November, and December). For either the general or subject tests, register early, especially if you plan to take the exam between November and January. There are provisions for fee waivers and for students with disabilities. To find out about them, contact your university's offices of financial aid and disability services, respectively. If you are out of school, talk to these same offices at a local public institution of higher learning.

TEST FORMAT: GENERAL TEST

The general test has three parts: verbal, quantitative, and analytical writing. The verbal section has 30 questions to be answered in 30 minutes. It is largely an exercise in critical reading. The quantitative section has 28 questions to be answered in 45 minutes. It requires a firm grasp of high school math: arithmetic, algebra, geometry, and data analysis. You do not need to know anything about calculus or trigonometry. The analytical writing section gives you 30 minutes to analyze an argument and 45 minutes to offer your perspective on an issue. The writing sections may be either handwritten or completed on a computer using simple word processing software.

For the computer adaptive test (CAT), the verbal and quantitative sections begin with a question of medium difficulty. A correct answer raises the bar; your next question will be harder. An incorrect answer has the opposite effect. In other words, you cannot skip a question and come back to it. Your score will depend on the difficulty and number of questions you answer correctly. Therefore, it is important to relax and concentrate on the early questions, which will dictate the later questions and the maximum score that you can achieve. Time is critical, so familiarity with the type of questions that may appear is very important. This is another reason to take a lot of practice tests.

For the issue section of analytical writing, you will choose between two topics to discuss. You will need to identify the central issue, define your terms, and provide arguments for or against it. You'll want to list arguments in support of your opinion. You'll give counterarguments and discuss where they apply in exceptional circumstances or where they are wrong. You get no choice of arguments in the second section. You will be expected to dissect the argument, give points pro and con, provide exceptions, and present possible counterarguments. For a complete list of possible topics, go to www.gre.org/pracmats.html. You will be graded on your organization, efficiency, focus, and analytical acuity, not on the stand you take with a particular issue. It's therefore a good idea to begin with an outline.

TEST FORMAT: SUBJECT TESTS

The paper-based subject test is offered in biology, chemistry, biochemistry and molecular biology, English literature, math, computer science, physics, and psychology. The areas tested within each of these disciplines are described in the GRE registration bulletin. Not all schools require a subject test score, but if you want to prove that you know more than what your undergraduate record suggests, or if you are changing fields, doing well on this test will help you make your point. You have about three hours to answer between 66 and 230 questions—depending on the test—of equal weight. One of the best ways to prepare for a subject test is to reread the text used in the first course (usually a survey course) you took in the subject. You'll be surprised by how much you have forgotten but equally surprised by how much you can easily relearn. And unlike the computer-based general test, subject tests are paper-based, so you can skip questions. Also unlike the general test, it takes four to six weeks for the scores to be mailed. If you need those scores to prove that you know the subject, make sure you take the test in plenty of time so that the score is with your application by the deadline.

What happens if the scores aren't as good as you had hoped for? You take the test again but prepare better this time. The graduate admissions committees will look at all of your scores, but in most cases they will concentrate on the most recent or the highest scores. If you don't prepare for the next test, however, you are wasting more of your time and money.

Once you get all of the GRE scores and your most recent cumulative GPA, you may want to eliminate from your list of schools a number of extreme long shots. Now you can start filling out the applications, which you can get in the mail by request or, in many cases, complete online. We have hundreds of grad school online applications available at www.PrincetonReview.com.

Test of English as a Foreign Language (TOEFL)

This four-hour test is required for entrance into more than 4,000 U.S. institutions of higher learning. Its purpose is to evaluate the oral comprehension and writing skills of students who do not use English as a primary language. The listening, structure, and reading sections of the examination are computer-adaptive. The writing section is not. The computer-based test is taken at regional test centers by appointment. For those who cannot get to the regional test center, paper tests are available five times a year. Be sure to register early for either test. To do well on the test, you must learn how it is structured, you must practice listening to and writing English, and you must know how to use your time wisely during the test. Basically, all the same principles apply to the TOEFL that apply to the GRE.

The test costs more than $100 and has all sorts of rules associated with the method and timing of payment. You can find more complete information concerning the TOEFL on the Web (www.toefl.org). You can send email to toefl@ets.org, call 609-771-7100, or write to TOEFL Services, ETS, PO Box 615, Princeton, NJ 08541-6151.

MCAT, GMAT, and LSAT

These are the entrance examinations for medical, graduate business, and law school, respectively. Since there are many more applications than there are total slots in these professional schools, you must do well on these tests to gain admissions to selective schools. The tests aren't cheap, either, which is a primary reason for being familiar with the test format and being prepared to answer technical questions.

The MCAT (Medical College Admissions Test) is a paper-based exam that is given twice a year (April and August) and requires traveling to a test center. If you want to go directly from college to medical school, the latest you can take the test is the summer between your junior and senior years of college. Administered over nine and a half hours, the MCAT tests your verbal capabilities with critical reading questions. Your knowledge of basic biology, chemistry, and physics will also be tested by multiple choice questions. You will have to compose two essays for the writing evaluation. For more information, online registration, and order forms for practice tests, visit the Association of American Medical Colleges (AAMC) at www.aamc.org/mcat.

The GMAT (General Management Admissions Test) is for admission to graduate programs in business. It is computer-adaptive (see the GRE section on page 26 for a description of this type of test), which means you must make an appointment to take the test at a center. The GMAT tests verbal, quantitative, and analytical writing skills.

Currently, you do not have to write an essay for the GMAT. For more information, visit www.gmat.org, or call 609-771-7330. The email address is gamt@ets.org, and the regular mailing address is GMAT, Distribution and Receiving Center, 225 Phillips Blvd., Ewing, NJ 08628-7435.

The LSAT (Law School Admission Test) is a four-hour, paper-based, multiple-choice test given about seven times a year. There are sections on reading comprehension, analytical reasoning, and logic. There is also an unscored writing section that admissions committees might use in making admissions decisions. For more information concerning registration and preparation materials, visit www.lsac.org or call 215-968-1001.

Completing the Application for Admission

THE GREAT EIGHT: CRUCIAL COMPONENTS OF YOUR GRADUATE SCHOOL APPLICATION

Let's state the obvious: If your application is incomplete or mailed after the published deadline for the program you're applying to, it won't be considered for admission or financial aid. Simple enough, you think, but to make your deadlines, you're going to have to exercise some planning and managerial finesse. Be sure to request transcripts and letters of recommendation a couple of months before your earliest deadline. Send in your application and fee two weeks before the deadline. Contact the department(s) on the deadline to make sure your file has been received and is complete. Since you're the type of person who would read up on grad school application strategies (you are reading this now), you're obviously conscientious. We're confident that you will make sure to meet all deadlines.

With that said, you need to keep some things in mind when completing your application, including your answers to some seemingly innocuous questions. Here's our advice on the eight components of your application that could trip you up if you don't attack them in the right way.

1. **Permanent Address.** If you're counting on in-state tuition at a public university for your survival in graduate school, your address is very important. If you are a full-time, non-tax-paying undergraduate student, this more likely than not means your parents' address (or whoever claims you as a dependent on their tax returns). Say your parents live in Kansas, but you don't want to go to school in the Sunflower State. You'd prefer to see the bright lights and tread the wide streets of Madison, Wisconsin (work with us here). Uncle Phil lives in Milwaukee. Why not just use his address? First, it's wrong, and this is no way to start an honorable career.

Second, Phil might think it's wrong and tell someone at the university that you are scamming them. If you didn't feel guilty before, you sure will now. Third, there already exists a long paper trail that indicates you have not been Uncle Phil's dependent. The legal and ethical way to change your permanent address is to move, establish residency, and *then* apply to graduate school.

2. **Degree Sought.** If your career aspirations require a PhD, then note that the degree you desire is a PhD. It doesn't matter if you don't already have a master's degree; most disciplines don't consider it a necessary prerequisite for a PhD program. Some fields, however, are exceptions to this rule; for example, theology PhD programs usually require a master's degree from some other institution in order for you to enroll. You may also feel that your academic credentials are not good enough—or too old—for you to be admitted to a PhD program. Applying for a master's program instead may indeed lower the bar for admission, but in many cases, if you're only applying for a master's degree in a program that also offers doctorates in the same discipline, your application will end up at the bottom of the acceptance and financial aid piles. It would be better to apply to a program that offers only a master's degree in your field.

3. **Financial Support.** Applications may ask if you want to be considered for financial aid. Unless you are independently wealthy, answer YES. This will not put your application at a disadvantage. Most applicants need financial aid in the form of tuition scholarships and stipends. *Admissions committees rank the applications on academic credentials and research interests, not financial need*. Some professional programs (law, business, and medical schools, for example) may have additional financial aid forms for you to complete for grants and loans.

4. **Personal Statement.** A graduate admissions committee looks for a few important items in a personal statement. First, the committee members want a measure of your writing skills. Applicants who cannot create an articulate and organized one-page statement using correct grammar and spelling will not be able to compose a 250-page dissertation. Use your writing software's grammar- and spell-checkers. Better than that, if you're still in college, get faculty members to look at the letter and press them for an honest critique. Pick a couple of friends who consistently tick you off with their frank honesty and ask if the statement makes sense. Stay away from "hard-sell" or cute approaches.

    Second, the committee is determining if the research area that you wish to study is available in their department. We have seen applicants with perfect GRE scores get rejected because their research interests did not match those of any faculty member. For example, you don't want to wax poetic about your ardent interest in sea cucumbers if there are no marine biologists on the faculty. You want to tell the committee enough for them to determine whether they have the research opening that meets your needs. This would be a good time to drop the name of a faculty member whose research interests you. (You've done your homework on this, haven't you?) Just make sure that the faculty member has not died, retired, or moved to another school. All you have to do to verify the viability of a potential advisor is call the department *before* you submit the application.

Third, the committee may be interested in your long-term career goals. Does the job you want really require a PhD? Are you really interested in experimental research, or do you just want the credentials to join a community mental health clinic (as a staff member, not a patient)?

Finally, the personal statement is a chance for you to explain the holes in your application. Why did you earn only a 2.2 GPA in your freshman year? Why do you want to study physics at the graduate level when your undergraduate major was archeology? What nonacademic life experiences will help you in your graduate studies?

Here's an example of what we mean. See if you can pick out an explanation of the applicant's lackluster GPA in the first two years of college, in what discipline the applicant is interested, what life experiences will contribute to his graduate studies, why the applicant is applying to this particular program, and what his long term career goal is.

> After two years of undergraduate survey courses, I was disillusioned with biology. But a course in parasitology, taught by Professor Frank Sogandares, changed all of that. He not only demanded a grasp of the vocabulary and concepts of the field; he also expected his students to use their imaginations to develop research questions and then go to the lab and the library to find their own answers. For the first time, I experienced research, and it was very stimulating.

> In my senior year, I took a graduate-level course taught by Prof. Sogandares that ended with the same result. Seven graduate students and I had to develop our own keys of digenetic trematodes and identify unknowns. We dissected muskrats and cottonmouths, looking for parasites. We never knew what to expect from class to class.

> Upon graduation, I was commissioned in the Navy. While on duty in the tropics, I collected blood samples from natives suffering from malaria and sent them back to my old professor. At the end of that tour, I knew that I wanted to go back to school to learn more about tropical diseases. I can't think of a better career than doing research and teaching students about what I have learned.

> The University of Massachusetts is an excellent place to study because there are three faculty members currently doing exciting research in parasitology. I am especially interested in the work of Professor Honigberg, who is working with the trypanosome that causes African sleeping sickness. Professor Nutting's work with parasitic arthropods is also interesting.

5. **Undergraduate Transcripts.** This is an essential item in your application package and one over which you have little control. Give your previous schools plenty of time—like a couple of months—to process your request for transcripts. Have the transcripts mailed directly to the appropriate address (i.e., where the rest of the application is being sent). Before the deadline, check with the department to which you're applying to make sure that the transcripts have arrived. If your GPA won't exactly cause the admissions committee to swoon with joy, then you need to explain (in your personal statement) why it doesn't reflect your ability and motivation to succeed in graduate school. A little evidence of your academic transformation might be in order. What was an intellectual turning point and how has this affected your most recent grades? What work have you done since graduation that has focused your career plans and galvanized your enthusiasm?

6. **Letters of Recommendation.** This is why those "how to get the most of college" books always tell you to get to know at least one professor a semester. And this is why you should have done undergraduate research and/or teaching assistance with a faculty member. These people will have something to say about your scholarly potential. Even if you have developed a good working relationship with one professor, you'll still need two other letters.

   For those recommendations, pick professors who have taught you recently and/or who have taught you more than once. Ask faculty who are well regarded in the field and who might know someone in the department you're applying to. Try to pick senior faculty. Finally, and most importantly, ask for letters of reference from professors who gave you an A in one of their classes.

   When you ask for a letter of reference, provide your referrer with a narrative summary of your undergraduate years describing what courses you liked and why and what research or practical experiences you have had. Explain why you want to go to graduate school and what your long-term career goals are. Also explain academic blemishes if necessary, but don't turn this piece into a mea culpa. If you have been out of college for several years, you should consider taking a couple of courses as a nondegree student just to have a current academic recommendation.

7. **Portfolio and Performance.** A portfolio of work often accompanies applications to fine arts programs (music performance, studio art, creative writing, theatre, architecture, etc.). Whether it is an audiotape, a videotape, a CD-ROM, paper, or 35mm slides, make sure that it is technically perfect. It won't matter that you are a virtuoso if your presentation is poor. The content of your portfolio should demonstrate both your command of the medium (technical skill) and ability to transcend the norm (imagination). Faculty members will be making admissions decisions, so don't think you're sending your portfolio to people who don't know what to look for. It's wise to provide a written explanation of your selection of pieces and the portfolio's overall theme. Performing artists will audition. Since you may have only 10 or 15 minutes in front of faculty members, be ready to perform and prepared to answer obvious questions. Why do you want to be an artist? Why did you choose this program in particular?

8. **Application Fees.** Pay them on time. And keep proof (cancelled checks, credit card statements, etc.) that you did.

How Your Application Will Be Evaluated

Usually a graduate admissions committee, made up of faculty members, decides whether you will be admitted and how much financial aid you will receive. That decision is based on your application, pressure from their fellow faculty members, the department's areas of expertise and needs, and the number of slots and financial aid dollars available. Sometimes, a campus interview is also a part of the selection process.

The committee ranks applications based on objective measures: undergraduate GPA, GPA in major and related fields, GRE general test scores, and GRE special test percentiles. But they will also weigh subjective criteria, like the quality of your undergraduate institution, your stated research interests and career goals, the strength of your letters of recommendation, the quality of the work in your portfolio, and undergraduate research or relevant work experience. Remember, however, that if your file is incomplete at the deadline, or if your fee is not paid, the committee will never even see your application.

A graduate admissions committee generally will not accept a student whose research interests are not represented in the department. You may also get rejected if you are interested in a research area that is already packed with graduate students. A call to the director of graduate studies or to a faculty member might save you from wasting time and money. It also helps to have a faculty member in your prospective department of choice who is in your corner. This is why a little homework goes a long way. Once you find out that there are faculty members who are doing research in an area that you find fascinating, an email to each asking if he or she would be interested in being your advisor is in order.

THE CAMPUS VISIT

You may be invited to campus. If this occurs before you get a letter of acceptance, this means you made the first cut but are still in the selection process. If this occurs after you have received an acceptance letter, the department is trying to recruit you. Either way, if the department invites you, they should be picking up the tab. If you receive an acceptance letter without an invitation to visit, call the department to ask if there is money available to fund your trip to campus. The visit is that important. It may be the difference between dropping out and graduating. At Notre Dame, the rate of graduate attrition dropped after the graduate school started providing money for campus visits because it gave applicants a chance to determine up-close if they would fit into the campus and departmental cultures.

You will be introduced to the faculty. Ask yourself: Are they really doing interesting research? Do they appear to be interested in you? How long does it take to get an advanced degree? What sort of jobs did the graduates get last year?

You will tour campus. Would you feel safe walking around it at night? Can you afford to rent a place off-campus? Are the computer clusters, library, and/or laboratory facilities adequate?

You will be introduced to graduate students. Honestly, are these people happy? (Granted, grad students aren't generally the happiest people around, but the majority of them shouldn't be completely miserable.) What are their workloads as teaching or research assistants? Are they surviving on their stipends? How do they support themselves during the summer? Does the school supplement medical insurance, and does the department provide professional development money? Are the students going to professional meetings and getting published?

Remember that what you see is the best the faculty and graduate students will behave. If you feel unconnected, ignored, or trampled (or all three) during your visit, then that's a sign.

If at First You Don't Succeed . . .

The best way to confront rejection is to ask those who denied you why they did so. It takes guts to call the director of graduate studies (DGS) and ask in a pleasant tone what your application was lacking. But that call will tell you where you can start improving. If it was your GRE score(s), you'll have plenty of time to prep and retake the test(s) before the next application deadline. If it was your undergraduate major or grade point average, then keep your day job and take a graduate course or two part-time to show that you can handle the material. If your research interests did not match those of the department, you need to do some homework to uncover the departments where they will. If the DGS says it was a combination of several factors, it means that you overreached in your selection of schools and you need to swallow your pride and go further down the rankings to find a home. If the DGS cannot point to anything and the directors in other departments say the same thing, you may have a poor letter of recommendation. It's time to find new faculty friends. Take a course in your field, do well, keep in touch, and ask the instructor to write a letter of recommendation during the next round. Take a job as a laboratory technician. Work hard and show aptitude. Then ask for a good letter of recommendation. We know more than one technician who ended up in *medical* school by playing that game.

Should you apply for the spring term in hopes that a slot becomes open? Probably not. All of the stipend and tuition money is given away in the fall term. Besides, it will take a year or more to build your credentials to the point that you become a top recruit deserving of support.

What to Expect and What Is Expected of You in Graduate School

No matter what the graduate program, you will spend the first two years doing course work. There may be only three to five courses per semester, but they will be advanced in nature and obviously important to your future as a professional. Not only is the material important, but the grade you receive in class will reflect the professor's opinion of your potential.

While you are concentrating on learning everything you can, you may also be assigned to teach for your stipend. To do a good job in front of a skeptical audience of undergraduates, you will have to learn far more than what you present in class or lab. If you multiply the number of course credits times five, you can estimate the out-of-class time it will take to prepare for the class and grade homework, quizzes, and papers. And at the end of the course, the students may get their turn grading your enthusiasm, organization, knowledge, and fairness. It's called the teacher/course evaluation. If you are enthusiastic and organized in your presentations and fair in your testing and grading, you will do fine.

Sometimes a qualifying exam is given during the first year to determine which courses you need to take. For professional degrees, you may have certification examinations at the end of the course of study. For research degrees, you will have written and oral examinations in your third or fourth year. You will have to propose and defend your research idea to a thesis or dissertation committee that you and your advisor have hand-picked to help you evaluate your research.

Finally, for a research master's degree or doctorate, you will do research. Coming up with an original idea (a question to which no one knows the answer) that isn't trivial takes time and considerable knowledge of a subject. You should be getting possible research topics during class and while studying for your comprehensive examinations. Write them down in a notebook before you forget them. Once you have the idea, you need to learn the techniques to answer the question. This will take two to many years depending upon your luck and skill. Finally, when you have it all figured out, you write the dissertation, which takes about a year.

While all of this appears to be hard (and it is), it will be fun. There is nothing like finding out something no one else has. It is very rewarding to see your name in print. If, on the other hand, you find graduate studies excruciating, there are many teaching jobs in small colleges that do not require much research. But you had better love to teach because you will be doing a lot of it.

What will be expected of you? Graduate school is career development, and by the time you walk across the stage to receive your diploma, you will have to prove to your future employer that you know a lot and can apply your knowledge. Faculty search committees look for evidence that you can teach the courses that need to be taught, do research, and interact with fellow faculty. Recruiters for government and industry will be more interested in evidence of teamwork and experience with specific research techniques. It's up to you to gather these credentials during the years you spend working toward your degree.

Viewing the Costs

Generally speaking, the costs associated with going to graduate school can be viewed in much the same way as those involved in securing a bachelor's degree. There are the tuition and fees to reckon with, as well as room and board, whether the student resides on or off campus. If you live on campus and eat meals provided by the institution, a bill is sent to you for these items each term. These costs are usually defined as "direct expenses." There are, of course, other costs—"indirect expenses"—not billed by the institution, but for which you will need to plan. These include books and supplies and a reasonable allowance for personal needs such as laundry, modest social expenses, and transportation. Since most graduate and professional students are considered self-supporting (no longer dependent on their parents), planning for additional indirect costs, especially for insurance, is important. Most institutions publish a standard "Costs of Attendance" document (sometimes also referred to as "Student Expense Budgets") both in their printed materials and on their websites. While these figures will vary from one school to the next because of varying tuitions and location (urban, suburban, rural; West Coast, East Coast, Midwest, South, etc.), there is typically an expectation and unwritten understanding that the indirect cost of attendance will be minimal because you will assume a more modest lifestyle.

PART 2

What's It Going to Cost?

Costs

Components of Cost of Attendance

- Tuition and fees
- Room and board*
- Books and supplies
- Personal expenses**
- Transportation

* Students residing in off-campus accommodations will need to include utilities in planning for room and board expenses.

** Personal expenses at the graduate or professional level should include the cost of medical insurance and care.

LOST OPPORTUNITY COSTS

As one considers the costs of attendance, which are likely to increase annually, it is important to weigh what economists refer to as "lost opportunity costs." In simple terms, if an individual were not enrolled in school, he or she would presumably otherwise be employed and earning income; therefore, part of the investment in graduate school is that which relates to these lost wages and any investments tied to those wages. Based upon the number of years one would not be working, this could be a significant cost consideration for some individuals, depending on their particular salaries and career paths. The primary consideration to keep in mind when weighing lost opportunity costs, however, is the fact that you are about to undertake an investment.

Education as an Investment

As can be argued for any costs associated with *any* form of instruction or training, advanced education and skills generally provide you with many long-term benefits. Most obvious among these are the enhanced economic prospects typically enjoyed by those with more education. Median family income statistics shed some light on the benefits of advanced education.

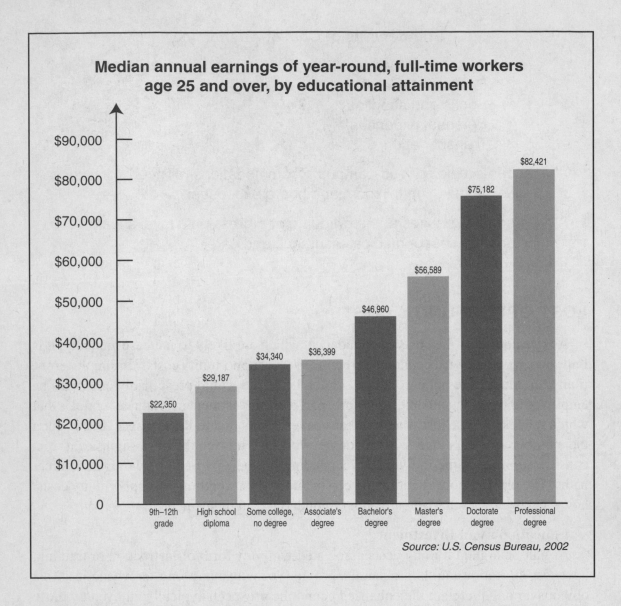

Median annual earnings of year-round, full-time workers age 25 and over, by educational attainment

Educational attainment	Median earnings
9th–12th grade	$22,350
High school diploma	$29,187
Some college, no degree	$34,340
Associate's degree	$36,399
Bachelor's degree	$46,960
Master's degree	$56,589
Doctorate degree	$75,182
Professional degree	$82,421

Source: U.S. Census Bureau, 2002

What is not as easily quantifiable in dollars and cents but is equally important in viewing the return on investment is a number of very real and lifelong benefits to both the individual and society. We'll discuss this point further in chapter 7. When one considers the broader, long-term view of these costs as an *investment* with typically major *returns*, the undertaking becomes less awesome and more reasonable.

LOANS

We discuss loans more exhaustively in chapter 7, including application procedures, eligibility criteria, limitations, sources of funds, lender selection, and repayment options. While that chapter will be focused on basic educational loan programs, a number of very basic points are noteworthy at this juncture.

Old-fashioned common sense would seem to suggest that borrowing to go to school, at any level of education, should be considered only as a last resort. Those in need of financial assistance to meet expenses should first seek things like fellowships, scholarships, and assistantships.

Securing student loans today is as easy as it has ever been. Not only are there ample opportunities through government-sponsored and privately financed programs, there are also very reasonable provisions for interest accrual and repayment. The entire application, delivery, and repayment processes have become very efficient and relatively simple through technological innovations. Moreover, the current IRS tax code provides eligible individuals with favorable tax considerations for the interest paid on educational loans, further reducing borrowing costs.

Characteristics
Professional and Graduate Students
1999/2000

- 88% of full-time, full-year students received aid.

- 60% of all students, including those studying less than full-time, received aid.

- Grants were the most common type of aid received.

- Loans constituted the largest dollar amounts of aid received.

- Doctoral students received larger grants on average ($13,372) than did master's ($7,606) or professional ($6,942) students.

- Professional students took out larger loans ($20,141) than did master's ($14,791) and doctoral ($14,085)students.

- Among full-time, full-year aid recipients, 50% of their total aid came from the federal government.

- About one-half of all students had taken out a Stafford loan as either an undergraduate or graduate student.

- Professional students borrowed the largest total amount ($48,742) compared to master's ($21,114) and doctoral ($33,055) students.

Source: U.S. Department of Education, National Center for Education Statistics, 1999-2000 National Postsecondary Student Aid Study

In addition to the standard government and private student loans, some individuals who may have been able to begin building equity in their homes, property, life insurance policies, and/or retirement programs, may be able to borrow from these resources under competitive terms and, again, sometimes with favorable tax considerations. Still others may be able to arrange even better deals through personal loans from family members or from employers. Individuals with these options would want to weigh the cost and risk involved with traditional student loans versus these other avenues. Often the best advice in reviewing such choices would be obtained from a tax accountant, banker, or personal finance specialist.

Regardless of the financing sought, good credit history is usually going to be a prerequisite. If you have outstanding student loans from undergraduate years and need to borrow more for graduate school, it would be wise to do so with the same lender. If this is not possible, then you should consider asking a new lender whether they would be willing to buy your student loan from the previous lender to help provide for a more coordinated repayment experience when payback time rolls round.

Finally, at least in respect to government-sponsored student loans, borrowers will be considered independent. Only the financial information of the applicant (and spouse, if married)—as opposed to that of the applicant and his or her parents—will be considered. While this is often the case for nongovernment loans as well, a few very selective, higher-cost private schools may, for their *institutional* financial assistance consideration, ask for parental financial information and cooperation as part of the application process. For individuals whose credit history is less than positive, lenders may require the co-signature of a creditworthy individual.

AID APPLICATION GENERAL HINTS

- Review the instructions. If certain questions are not clear, ask a school official.

- Have the appropriate tax year documents available. You'll probably need them.

- Respond completely, accurately, and legibly to all required questions. If certain information requested is not applicable or requires a zero response, be sure to indicate NA or -0- rather than leaving the answer blank.

- Meet deadlines. Most institutions will not set aside resources for late applicants.

- If you have any special circumstances that warrant mention, send them to the institution in a format that clearly indicates your full name and identification information, the same way it appears in all other correspondence sent to the institution. Attaching any addenda to a form (e.g., the FAFSA) on which there is no accommodation for referencing special circumstances will serve only to delay the processing of that particular form.

- If there is a request for any additional information or documentation during the application process, be sure to respond immediately and completely.

- Check to ensure that the application has been received by the organization to which you sent it. Web technology usually provides up-to-date access to such basic applicant status.

Expectations

One of the biggest frustrations in trying to find the resources necessary to make graduate or professional education affordable is that faced by those who come to the plate with the challenge of meeting *more* than the institution's standard cost of attendance. Certainly, reasonable adjustments are included for students who also have dependents or other obligations. Accommodating other financial responsibilities incurred for discretionary decisions made before or during graduate or professional school will often bring very difficult (i.e., expensive), if not insurmountable, challenges. Ideally, other than for previous student loans which typically can be deferred again when returning to school, the student's financial slate is clean. This would assume no excessive credit card or automobile payments and no other such serious financial obligations. Standard cost of attendance budgets, while including modest allowances for personal and transportation costs, do not include major additional expenses unrelated to basic educational needs. We strongly recommended that individuals hoping to return to school first eliminate these monthly expenses *before* they enroll, as attempting to deal with them while in school could quickly become problematic. Distractions, especially financial distractions, from your primary focus—school—are unnecessary. In the worst scenario, overly burdensome financial obligations could lead to premature withdrawal from school. So at least while in school, maintaining a frugal lifestyle is crucial. A classic line often heard in orientation sessions for law students applies to all graduate and professional school students: "If you live like a lawyer while you're a law student, you will live like a law student when you are a lawyer."

More can and will be said later (in chapter 8) on the related issue of money management and budgeting while you are in school.

Graduate and Professional School

It is important to note that the process and policies for graduate school students will typically be somewhat different from those that professional school students (law, medicine, dentistry, business, health, etc.) will face. While there may be some exceptions, generally speaking, a graduate student seeking a PhD would hope to receive some level of institutional support through fellowships and assistantships.

Sources of Aid
Professional and Graduate Students
1999–2000

- Professional students received larger amounts of federal aid than other graduate students, on average ($17,579 compared to $13,037 for doctoral students and $11,527 for master's students).

- MBA students were more likely than other master's students to receive aid from their employers.

- PhD students (except those in education) were more likely to receive institutional aid than other doctoral students.

- Professional students were more likely than students in other degree programs to rely solely on the federal government for financial aid.

Source: U.S. Department of Education, National Center for Education Statistics, 1999–2000 National Postsecondary Student Aid Study

---

Fellowships and assistantships may often require the student to serve as a graduate, teaching, or research assistant. The support can range from partial assistance toward tuition to full tuition and fees, as well as a monthly stipend. As noted in chapter 5, the value of a stipend could vary by the academic discipline and, to a lesser degree, by geographic location. Some disciplines have going rates determined by the nature of the particular course of study.

On the other hand, professional students can generally be expected to receive smaller levels of direct institutional assistance. While there may be exceptions based upon the truly outstanding credentials of a candidate or the student's disadvantaged background, most professional school students won't receive full scholarships covering all of their expenses, or even all of their tuition. Monthly stipends are also not typically provided. Scholarships may indeed be awarded, but it's common for professional students—even the truly exceptional ones—to take on some amount of student loans to pay the bills.

Employment
Professional and Graduate Students
1999/2000

- 63% of full-time, full-year students were employed for an average of 26 hours per week.

- Professional students were less likely to work while enrolled (45%) than master's (71%) or doctoral (67%) students.

- Of the 43% of students who were married, 93% had a spouse with an income averaging $37,998.

Source: U.S. Department of Education,
National Center for Education
Statistics, 1999–2000 National
Postsecondary Student Aid Study

Borrowing heavily for certain professional degrees is also not at all uncommon and it is not unusual for students holding the highest degrees to have incurred the largest level of student debt. On the other hand, to keep things in perspective, such students also have often been in school for more years and have had to face more expenses. Moreover, despite some exceptions, professional school graduates are typically those whose earning potential will be larger and more capable of handling the additional debt. At least, this is the justification institutions often use to loan you someone else's money rather than give you their own.

PART 3

How to Pay for It

Types of University Aid

According to a recent National Center for Education Statistics (NCES) study, the average budget for a full-time graduate student at a public university was about $19,200 for a master's student; $22,600 for a PhD student; and $24,000 for a student in professional school. Add $12,000 if the student is attending a private university. This figure includes, for both public and private schools, $13,210 a year in non-tuition-related expenses.

You know that grad school will cost you money in terms of lost income. And you know that deferred gratification may pay off big time if you obtain a law, medical, or professional master's degree. So the loan payments you eventually make will be a business expense. A PhD takes longer to obtain than a law or business degree, and the salaries—certainly the starting salaries—in academia are less than those in the private sector. Pursuing a nonprofessional graduate degree, however, is all about job satisfaction, and that should be your most important consideration. This doesn't mean that you should mortgage the rest of your life following your dreams. But to right a lopsided cost-benefit ratio, you need to reduce the expenses associated with going to graduate school. The best way to do that is to find someone else who will pay your tuition and provide you with a stipend and money to do your research. In the 1999–2000 academic year, more than 80 percent of full-time graduate and professional degree students received some form of financial aid totaling an average of $19,521 each. Here's how and where they got it.

The biggest source of financial aid for grad school comes from the university that you are applying to and the faculty who work there. The more they want you, the more of their resources they will offer you. Here are some of the types of offers that you may receive; a few dollars may be just for showing up, a few you may have to work for, and a few you may have to pay back.

Tuition Scholarships and Waivers

For professional degrees (e.g., law, MBA, medical, engineering), this may be all you can expect, and you may receive only partial tuition support. The rest of your education will have to be paid for by campus employment, savings, spousal income, and/or loans.

In the 1999–2000 academic year, 46 percent of full-time master's and professional students received about $7,300 in scholarships each, versus 62 percent of doctoral students, who received an average scholarship of $13,400. You do not have to pay back scholarship money, and most of the time you don't have to work for it either. If the scholarship has no service requirement, it is not considered taxable income. Therefore, it should not appear on W-2 or 1099 forms, and you do not have to report it on your annual 1040. You do not have to report it when applying for loans or state aid. Obviously, however, you can't claim the tuition bill covered by the scholarship as an educational expense, either. Occasionally, some bureaucrat will try to add your scholarship as income. If that happens, you should then demand that the tuition bill be added as an expense. Then the two wash, and everyone is happy. If work is required for your tuition scholarship or waiver, the money may be considered taxable income. Be sure that you have in writing what work—if any—you need to do for scholarship money.

Generally, tuition scholarships are Monopoly money, good for internal transactions only. In other words, if you get a $15,000 scholarship but decide to take only $10,000 worth of courses, you cannot collect $5,000 to pay the rent (even if it's campus housing).

Sometimes, state schools find it easier not to bill someone than to find scholarship money because state legislatures are very tight with tax dollars—hence the invention of tuition waivers. You are simply not billed for the courses taken, or the additional out-of-state tuition charge may be waived. Sometimes partial tuition scholarships are called fellowships. You receive a cash award that is promptly subtracted from your tuition bill. There probably will be no money left over to pay the electric bill.

Stipends

There are two major ways that you earn a student stipend: by teaching for a department or by doing research for a faculty member. The percentage of students who receive stipends and the amount paid to each will vary depending on intended degree and field (see the table below), enrollment status (full- or part-time), and years of enrollment. A small number of students may get a stipend just for showing up (i.e., recipients of fellowship holders).

Stipends, Tuition Scholarships, and Fringe Benefits for the Average Graduate Student in 1999-2000

Degree Sought		Teaching assistant		Research assistant		% of TA/RA receiving some	
		% of students	Stipend	% of students	Stipend	Benefits	Tuition
MA	Arts and Letters	32%	$7,300	8%	$8,300	33%	67%
	Science and Engineering	32%	$7,300	39%	$8,300	37%	75%
	Education	8%		3%		7%	42%
	MBA	11%		11%		21%	41%
PhD	Arts and Letters	41%	$9,200	18%	$8,400	52%	74%
	Science and Engineering	34%	$10,000	58%	$12,300	55%	80%
	Education	17%		13%		26%	63%

GRADUATE/TEACHING ASSISTANTS (GA/TA)

In return for nine months of career-related work, you will be paid a stipend to cover your living and otherwise uncovered educational expenses. A stipend may be associated with a title: full-time graduate assistant, half-time teaching assistant, etc. The title will vary; the important things to know are how many hours you are supposed to work and for how many dollars per semester.

A stipend is supposed to allow students the time to devote their full attention to their studies instead of having to flip burgers to pay the rent. If, however, you are married with children and trying to get a master's in art history in downtown Boston, survival on a stipend alone is unlikely. You will need to know the cost of living within the school's locale for you and your dependents. If there is a gap between stipend and fiscal reality, ask the director of graduate studies what students do to make ends meet and how many hours a week they need to do it.

You also need to know how many academic years you are guaranteed a stipend, assuming satisfactory academic progress. Of course, your next question should be: What is the average time it takes students in your discipline to earn a degree? There may be a gap in funding between the two, and you need to ask the director of graduate studies how students support themselves after the assistantship runs out.

The career-related work associated with the stipend should add luster to your curriculum vitae. Less experienced teaching assistants will supervise course laboratories, grade examinations, give guest lectures in class, run tutorials, or lead discussion sections. More senior graduate assistants may actually design their own courses and give all of the lectures.

Be a Persistent Assistant

If you are planning an academic career, get as much experience as you can assisting with a variety of courses in your discipline. It not only looks good to a faculty search committee; it gives you ready-made courses or laboratories for when you start your career. You can, however, spend too much time developing courses instead of doing your dissertation research (which, by the way, is your only ticket out). Find out how much class time you will be expected to work for the stipend, and then multiply it by three to cover the work that you will have to do to prepare for the class for the first time and grade the work that is generated during class. If it is more than 20 hours of total preparation and class time, you will have a difficult time teaching, completing your own course work, and doing your dissertation research.

The amount of stipend money that you receive will vary among schools, among departments within a school, and even among students within the department. This academic fact of life extends to faculty contracts as well. It is more important for you to determine if the stipend is enough to keep you out of significant debt in the short run than to wonder why your next-door neighbor is making more money than you are.

The amount of stipend may be independent of the amount of time you put in. On average, graduate students put in about 16 hours a week toward TA duties, but this varies from a low of 14 hours (in the classroom) for humanities students to an average of 20 hours per week (in the 3- to 4-hour teaching labs) for scientists.

The stipend is taxable income (federal, state, county, and city), and if you are classified as an employee, you may also lose part of your paycheck to that guy FICA. It is important to know how much of your earnings will disappear before you get your paycheck.

You may be expected to pay school fees, supplies, and books out of your stipend, as well as tuition. Don't forget medical insurance and health center fees along with parking, technology, and general student activity fees. Then there are the normal living expenses of room, board, and transportation. There won't be much left over for entertainment, but take solace in the fact that your classmates won't have time or money for high times, either. But hey, you're an imaginative person. Think of cheap, fun things to do in the limited time that you have to party.

How do you get a teaching assistantship? You answer "yes" to the question on your application that reads, "Do you wish to be considered for financial aid?" If the department has the money, it will offer assistantships to its best applicants.

RESEARCH ASSISTANTS

Research assistants get a stipend for doing research for a faculty member. The amount of the funding will vary depending upon the discipline (see the table on page 61). The source of your stipend as a research assistant may be a government grant or the university coffers. But it's all legal tender. Grants require frequent renewal to keep the money flowing, so this route may appear risky. But university RA money is not guaranteed, either.

Generally, in social sciences and humanities, you will be helping faculty members with their research. The more you pay attention, get involved, and ask questions, the more you will learn about the research process. The methods that you learn will come in handy when you approach your own dissertation.

In science and engineering, on the other hand, your dissertation research will most often contribute data to the overall research goals of your graduate advisor. In other words, you will be paid as a research assistant to do your own dissertation. The downside is that you may find yourself on a data assembly line where it will be difficult to get involved with the planning and publication ends of the research. In order to avoid becoming a lab technician instead of a researcher, you will need to assert yourself and get involved with the generation of ideas, the planning of experiments, and the writing of grant proposals and journal articles.

Sounds good! Where do I sign up? In general, the faculty members who get the research grants hand out research assistantships. Therefore, if the faculty member happens to be your graduate advisor, you will be first in line. Even if your advisor doesn't have any research dollars, another faculty member may. Sometimes, researchers have extra work or special needs (e.g., translations, Webwork, statistical analysis, etc.). Such piecework will probably not support you completely, but it will be a nice career-enhancing supplement to your income.

In general, research assistantships pay more than teaching assistantships. This is no doubt due to the fact that new students in science and engineering are given the teaching responsibilities, while the more advanced students are awarded research assistantships. Both have their advantages. The TA gives you teaching experience; the RA gives you research experience. The best of all possible graduate student worlds will involve both.

FELLOWSHIPS

Receiving a fellowship is an honor. Every academic department, however, will have a different definition of what a fellowship is. Do not assume anything. How many years does this fellowship last? What happens after it expires? Is the stipend for 12 months or 9? Is a full tuition scholarship included? Does the tuition scholarship include summer courses? What fees and benefits, especially health insurance and on-campus parking, are covered? What work do you have to perform for the fellowship and for how long? Does a research allowance come with the fellowship? A research allowance that can be used to purchase equipment (e.g., a computer) and books or travel to professional meetings is an increasingly popular recruiting perk. It pays for many hidden professional development costs, but it is not considered income so Uncle Sam does not get a chunk of it. The research allowance is not a common feature for most university fellowships, but it may be available with certain federal fellowships (like the NSF Graduate Fellowships, Javits Fellowships, and others).

The best fellowships will last for three to five years and include a 12-month stipend. There should be more stipend money and less work than what a TA is required to perform.

But don't be surprised if TAs, especially on unionized campuses, get more benefits, health insurance, parking, special book rates, and office space than fellows. Subtract their benefits from your fellowship stipend to determine if they get the better deal.

You may think that getting money for nothing is the best of all possible deals, but that isn't necessarily the case. Surely, having totally unobstructed time to study and do research will improve your grades and should reduce your time-to-degree. However, Barbara Lovitts, author of *Leaving the Ivory Tower: The Causes and Consequences of Departure from Doctoral Study*, claims that multiyear, service-free fellowships are a recipe for disaster because fellows have a difficult time socially integrating themselves into the departmental culture without the work-related contact with faculty and fellow students. Furthermore, when you prepare lectures or laboratories, you learn the subject at a much deeper level than if you were sitting on the other side of the lectern taking the notes. The final argument against service-free fellowships is that a graduate with no teaching experience is at a disadvantage when applying for a faculty position. The faculty search committee will wonder about your pedagogical skills. And even if they hire you, you will arrive on campus with no lectures or laboratories already prepared. For one 50-minute lecture, it can take five hours of research to produce three to five pages of double-spaced information. And a new assistant professor is expected to come up with three lectures a week for 14 weeks for one to three different courses!

Why offer fellowships if there are so many possible downsides? Because they appear attractive to *you*. How do you mitigate the possible problems associated with multiyear fellowships? First, you find out if and when there is a teaching requirement. If there is none, then you might volunteer your services to the director of graduate studies. What's really nice about a fellowship is that you are in a position to set the limits of your volunteer service. Teaching a semester of a course that you know you will teach as an assistant professor is a good deal. Teaching different courses each semester also broadens your experience. It will be an easy sell, since directors of graduate studies always need help. Of course, if you missed your calling as a haggler in an Turkish bazaar, you might even negotiate additional money or benefits for teaching a course.

So how do you get in line for this free university fellowship money? Unlike fellowships awarded by foundations or the government, there usually is no separate application. The department will nominate you based on your application to graduate studies. Don't assume anything, though, and ask the director of graduate studies if there is anything you need to do to apply for a university fellowship.

Other Forms of Campus Employment

Stipends can pay well. Let's assume that you get a $10,000 teaching assistantship for the academic year (about 30 weeks), which requires about 20 hours of work per week. This comes to a rate of $16.67 per hour. It would be difficult to match this by working part-time on or off campus. The closest you could get would be to become a dormitory/floor manager. Sometimes these jobs provide free room and board, a stipend, and/or tuition remission. The bad news is that you work far more than 20 hours a week and often at unpredictable and inconvenient times. And unless you are planning on becoming a clinical psychologist, a minister, or a prison guard, this is not exactly job-related experience. It does pay the bills, however, and many professional school students line up for these few jobs.

If you need a campus job, find the student employment office. Many departments need low-tech level clerical staff. If you bring significant technical skills (language, computer, laboratory, statistical), hit both the student employment office and departments that could use your particular expertise. Sometimes, the department or researcher will pay you your entire wage; sometimes the federal government pays part of it (work-study programs). To you, the source won't matter.

Also check out the university's human resources department, which hires full-time and part-time employees. If you show up on campus with skills like law enforcement, firefighting, information technology, or experimental methods, you may land high-paying part-time jobs in academic support. Sometimes being a university employee provides more benefits (including some tuition remission) and better salary than student employment. It may mean, however, that you become a full-time employee and a part-time student, which will prolong your time-to-degree.

Money for Research

So you manage to get a tuition scholarship and even a stipend that will cover your tuition and living expenses for the year. What more do you possibly need? How about the cost of research? For most experimentalists (scientists, psychologists, and engineers, for example), your project will probably be possible to complete using solely the supplies and equipment already in the lab of your graduate advisor. Most students in the humanities cover their research costs with a library card. But what if you need a piece of equipment or supplies for experiments that your advisor cannot afford? What if you need to buy a database or go to a distant workshop to learn how to work the software and statistically analyze the data? What if you need to travel to an archive or a site in order to see something that cannot be found on campus or on the Internet? In these cases, you end up doing the same thing that a faculty member does when confronted with the same questions: You find someone who also wants to know the answer to your research question and is willing to pay for it. More than likely, this someone will be an off-campus foundation or government agency, but you should not overlook less competitive opportunities at your school. Ask your graduate advisor, your director of graduate studies, and the campus research office what local research grant opportunities exist.

Professional Development

Graduate school is all about getting a job after graduation. And for research positions (academic or industrial), it is the research you produce in school that is one of your most important credentials. Your research record includes presentations of your results at professional meetings and journal publications. It costs money to travel to and participate in professional meetings. Journal articles have page charges. Who pays for this? If your graduate advisor has grant support, he or she may foot the bill. Otherwise, you will have to look to your department, the academic dean, the university research office, or the graduate school. There may also be outside sources of support.

Types of Nonuniversity Aid

Fellowships

Extramural fellowships—that is, awards that don't come from faculty research grants or university coffers—are funding sources for which you apply directly independent of the school. Some of the largest extramural fellowships come from the government; some of the most prestigious come from private foundations. Some support you for several years, others for just one year while you're getting started, doing field research, or writing your dissertation. A few fellowships even support a year of travel between college and graduate school. There are, however, few fellowships offered by foundations or the government that apply to students in professional schools or in master's degree programs.

Extramural fellowships usually supply a healthy stipend and a partial or full tuition scholarship. Sometimes you'll also get an educational allowance. Because you are supported by an institution or organization outside of the university, you shouldn't have to teach or do research for a faculty member. Some fellowships will, however, have an academic requirement to teach courses sometime during your graduate career. What better way to learn how to do research than to assist faculty in their research? But because you are bringing in your own stipend and at least some tuition, you are in a good position to negotiate with departments.

Negotiate what? First, you can discuss what courses you want to teach, how many times, and when. Second, you get to pick the faculty that you want to assist with research. Third, even a four-year fellowship will not cover your entire stay as a graduate student. Remember that the average time-to-degree for a PhD is about six years, even if all goes well. So you need to find out how much the department will guarantee you when the fellowship runs out. Finally, you need to negotiate the institutional allowance that may accompany the fellowship. Often, universities put that money toward your tuition. But if everyone else in the department is being covered by departmental scholarships or waivers, you should ask if your educational allowance could be set aside to cover your other expenses, such as fees, health insurance, course books, school supplies, research equipment, or professional travel. This untaxed benefit will definitely put you into the highest of graduate student income brackets, which will almost approach the poverty level for a family of four. Sometimes departments will buy your ideas concerning the educational allowance, sometimes the fellowship sponsor defines exactly what the money is to be spent for, and sometimes the university has a different view on how the money should be spent. It's in your best interest to ask, and it will be an interesting point to consider when negotiating with more than one department concerning their offers of admission.

Below are listed the types of fellowships accompanied by some prominent examples. This is by no means an exhaustive list. There are books in the reference section of your school library, research office, and/or career and placement offices that list even more.

The Internet is also a valuable resource, but many of the easy-to-use searchable databases require school membership for access.

The trick to working with searchable databases is not to be so general that hundreds of irrelevant funding possibilities are listed or so specific that hardly any are listed at all. The best strategy is to start by ignoring deadline, amount of award, or type of sponsor and concentrate on a general area of research interest (e.g., search for "archeology," not "excavation of St. Steven's monastery") and type of award (graduate fellowship, travel grant, etc.). If you get many listings and most appear to be irrelevant, be more selective with the description of your research topic.

When searching through books or databases, remember that your topic may be interdisciplinary and attractive to many different agencies. For instance, your desire to study the causes and effects of the persecution of the Huguenots might interest agencies that fund projects in religious studies, history, or American studies. Your research may be applied to all of their causes. And keep in mind that many disciplines may be listed in several categories. For example, history may be considered in some databases as a social science and in others as a field in the humanities; political theory may be found in political science or philosophy; environmental studies may also be found in engineering, biology, natural resources, wildlife or forest management, or ecology.

Bridge Support Between College and Graduate School

You apply for these awards at the beginning of your senior year in college to attend a foreign university for a year or two. These are just four of the best-known and biggest awards.

Marshall Scholarships

You need a 3.7 GPA as a senior to apply for a Marshall Scholarship. The $25,000 stipend is in addition to a travel and expense allowance to attend a British graduate school for one or two years.

Email: info@marshallscholarship.org

Website: www.marshallscholarship.org

Fulbright Grants and Teaching Assistantships

There should be a Fulbright advisor on your campus who will have information and applications for this prestigious grant. You apply early in your senior year. The grants send you to campus in 1 of 140 countries to take courses, so you need to know the local language. You can also teach American studies in high schools in Belgium, Luxembourg, France, Germany, Hungary, Korea, Romania, Taiwan, or Turkey.

Phone: 212-984-5327

Email: wjackson@iie.org

Website: www.iie.org/TemplateFulbright.cfm?section=Fulbright1

Rhodes Scholarships

A Rhodes Scholarship provides tuition, fees, and maintenance costs for two to three years of graduate work at Oxford University. Only 32 awards to American students are given each year, so you have to be very, very good. See your campus advisor or academic dean if you are interested.

Email: amsec@rhodesscholar.org

Website: www.rhodesscholar.org

Rotary International Ambassadorial Scholarships

Rotary Ambassadorial Scholarships are one- and two-year fellowships for study abroad to foster international understanding among people of different countries.

Phone: 847-866-3326

Email: scholarshipinquiries@rotaryintl.org

Website: www.rotary.org/foundation/educational/amb_scho/index.html

Multiyear Fellowships

These fellowships may run from two to five years for pre-doctoral studies. The stipend is usually enough to spread over 12 months. Sometimes, an educational allowance and/ or a tuition scholarship are included. Most require U.S. citizenship and an intention to obtain a PhD. The fellowships that seniors in college and junior graduate students apply for require only a general idea about a particular research topic—about as much as you would need for your letter of intent that accompanies your application for admission. Of course, a first- or second-year student will usually have a better-formed idea, plus graduate experience.

Some of the most prestigious multiyear fellowships offered by the federal government and large foundations are briefly described below. Most require you to apply during your senior year of college or first year in graduate school.

American Psychological Association Minority Fellowship Program

This three-year fellowship provides a $12,000 stipend and travel allowance to students studying mental health, AIDS, or substance abuse services.

Phone: 202-336-6127

Email: mfp@apa.org

Website: www.apa.org/mfp

American Society of Mechanical Engineers Graduate Teaching Fellowships

These are awarded to those pursuing a doctorate in mechanical engineering with the goal of an academic career. Stipends are for $5,000 per year.

Phone: 212-591-8131

Email: oluwanifieset@asme.org

Website: www.asme.org/education/enged/aid/fellow.htm

American Society for Microbiology Watkins Minority Graduate Fellowships

These awards are three years of stipend support ($19,000 per year) for a member of specified minority group who is studying microbiology.

Phone: 202-942-9283

Email: fellowships-careerinformation@asmusa.org

Website: www.asm.org/Education/index.asp?bid=6278

American Sociological Association Minority Fellowship Program

This three-year, up to $19,968 per year stipend supports minority sociology graduate students who are interested in doing research in mental health.

Email: minority.affairs@asanet.org

Website: www.asanet.org/student/mfp.html

Dolores Zohrab Liebmann Fellowships

This is a three-year fellowship ($18,000 stipend per year) for graduate students with exceptional undergraduate records who are studying almost anything. It is best to apply for this award after a year or two of graduate school. It requires a nomination by the dean of the graduate school, who should contact the sponsor on your behalf.

Website: www.fdncenter.org/grantmaker/liebmann/

Ford Foundation Pre-doctoral Fellowships for Minorities

These are four-year fellowships carrying an annual $17,000 stipend and cost-of-education allowance for African Americans, Native Americans, and selected groups of Hispanic Americans, available at the beginning of their graduate education.

Phone: 202-334-2872

Email: infofell@nas.edu

Website: www7.nationalacademies.org/fellowships/fordpredoc.html

The Fund for Theological Education Fellowships for African Americans

Applicants must be interested in earning a PhD in religious or theological studies, committed to providing leadership within theological education, and strongly considering a career in seminary teaching and research. The stipend is $15,000.

Phone: 404-727-1450

Email: sfluker@thefund.org

Website:www.thefund.org/programs/fellowships/doctoral/index.html

The Fund for Theological Education Ministry Fellowships

These support MDiv students during their studies for the professional degree. The award includes a $5,000 stipend and travel allowance.

Phone: 404-727-1450

Email: mwigint@thefund.org

Website: www.thefund.org/programs/fellowships/ministry/index.html

Graduate Education for Minorities (GEM) MS and PhD Fellowships

These are three-semester fellowships for minority students in engineering and science. They pay a $10,000 to $14,000 stipend and some tuition at a GEM member university and get students internships during the summer.

Website: www.gemfellowship.org

International Foundation for Ethical Research: Alternatives in Scientific Research

This is an up to three-year fellowship that also has a research supply fund. It includes a $12,500 stipend and a $2,500 supply allowance. Your research must involve issues of animal welfare in research, product testing, and education.

Phone: 312-427-6025

Email: ifer@navs.org

Website: www.ifer.org

Jacob Javits Fellowship

The U.S. Department of Education administers this award, which provides up to four years of stipend support (up to $30,000 per year) plus a $11,511 educational allowance to PhD-intents in the humanities. You must apply before your second year of graduate school.

Phone: 202-502-7542

Email: OPE_Javits_Program@ed.gov

Website: www.ed.gov/programs/iegpsjavits/index.html

Link Foundation Energy Fellowship Program

These are two-year fellowships ($25,000 annual stipend) for PhD students who are doing research with societal energy supply and use.

Phone: 603-646-2231

Website: www.linkenergy.org

National Aeronautics and Space Administration (NASA) Graduate Student Researchers Program

This program provides up to three years of stipend support (up to $24,000 annually) for engineering or science students whose research interests are compatible with NASA programs.

Phone: 202-358-0402

Email: kblandin@hq.nasa.gov

Website: http://fellowships.hq.nasa.gov/gsrp/program/

National Defense Science and Engineering Graduate Fellowships

This three-year fellowship is intended for engineering and science students at the beginning of their graduate careers. The stipend increases each 12-month period by $500, and currently the annual award is $27,500. The institutional allowance for this fellowship goes for tuition only. If you don't have health insurance, the Department of Defense will pay for minimal coverage, up to $1,000 per year.

Phone: 202-331-3516

Email: ndseg@asee.org

Website: www.asee.org/ndseg/

National Institutes of Health (NIH) Pre-doctoral Training Grants

These grants provide multiyear support in several medically related biological and mental health fields for U.S. citizens, with some specifically for U.S. minority students. The award carries an $11,500 stipend and a $2,000 education allowance.

Phone: 301-435-0714

Email: GrantsInfo@nih.gov

Website: http://grants1.nih.gov/grants/index.cfm

National Institutes of Health Pre-doctoral Training Grant in Bioinformatics and Computational Biology

This is a three-year fellowship with a $14,688 stipend.

Phone: 301-594-0828

Email: cassattj@nigms.nih.gov

Website: http://grants1.nih.gov/grants/index.cfm

National Physical Science Consortium Graduate Fellowships in Physical Science

These fellowships provide six years of support for students who want to study engineering, math, or physical sciences at a member institution. The stipend is $16,000 per year.

Phone: 213-243-2409

Email: npsc@npsc.org

Website: www.npsc.org

National Science Foundation (NSF) Graduate Research Fellowships

This is a three-year fellowship with a hefty cost-of-education allowance for graduate students in science, social sciences, and engineering. Humanities students in the history or philosophy of science may also apply. The window for applying starts in your senior year in college and stretches to the beginning of your second year of graduate school. Applications must be completed online. Recipients have five years to spend the money.

Phone: 866-353-0905

Website: www.nsf.gov/pubs/2003/nsf03050/nsf03050.htm

Social Sciences and Humanities Research Council of Canada Fellowships

These fellowships provide multiyear support for Canadian students studying several different research topics, including Canadian studies, the new economy, and medieval history. The award is worth up to $17,500 per year in Canadian dollars.

Phone: 613-992-0691

Email: webgrant@sshrc.ca

Website: www.sshrc.ca

Soros Fellowships

These are three-year fellowships to support new Americans in any field of graduate study. The award includes a $20,000 stipend and a grant of one-half of the tuition of the graduate program you are attending. You must be under 30 and have a green card or be a naturalized citizen or be the child of naturalized parents.

Phone: 212-547-6926

Email: pdsoros_fellows@sorosny.org

Website: www.pdsoros.org

U.S. Environmental Protection Agency (EPA) STAR Graduate Environmental Fellowships

These fellowships provide multiyear support for either master's or PhD students to do research in environment-related fields. The award includes a $20,000 stipend, $5,000 educational allowance, and $5,000 international activities allowance and up to $12,000 tuition scholarship, all awarded annually.

Phone: 800-490-9194

Website: http://es.epa.gov/ncer/fellow/

First-Year and Dissertation Research Fellowships and Grants

Doing research costs money. You may need to travel to distant archives, archeological sites, or other research laboratories. For this you will need not only travel money, but a stipend that doesn't require you to teach three times a week. Perhaps you need to purchase research materials, such as a government database, computer hardware or software, or exotic chemicals. Maybe you just need some uninterrupted time (i.e., no service requirements attached to the stipend) to collect your thoughts and/or data, analyze the material, or write your dissertation.

In order for you to win the following extramural fellowships, you have to demonstrate in your applications a clear idea of what your dissertation project will be, and it must contain a feasible and valid plan of action toward achieving your research goal. Therefore, PhD students are generally not ready to apply for these awards until their third or fourth year, after completing their courses and oral comprehensive examinations.

The fellowships and grants listed below are divided into four categories based on discipline. All of them provide enough money for stipends; most will have additional allowances. There are far more entries for arts and letters students than scientists and engineers because graduate advisors will support most of the latter.

Cross-Discipline Fellowships

These fellowships attract applications from scientists, humanists, engineers, and social scientists.

American Association of University Women (AAUW) Dissertation Fellowships are one-year, $20,000 fellowships for female U.S. citizens at the dissertation-writing stage. The AAUW also awards one-year fellowships of $5,000 to $12,000 to women who are entering master's or first professional programs in disciplines in which women's participation traditionally has been low.

Phone: 800-326-AAUW

Email: aauw@act.org

Website: www.aauw.org/fga/fellowships_grants/american.cfm

American Center for Oriental Research Fellowships are for scientists, social scientists, or humanities students hoping to address topics concerning the Near East. Stipends are up to $19,400. You must be a U.S. citizen to be considered.

Phone: 617-353-6571

Email: acor@bu.edu

Website: www.bu.edu/acor

American-Scandinavian Foundation Awards provide $18,000 stipends or $3,000 grants to study in one of the Scandinavian countries for a year.

Phone: 212-879-9779

Email: info@amscan.org

Website: www.amscan.org

Dartmouth College Cesar Chavez and Thurgood Marshall Fellowships are one-year residential minority fellowships supporting study at Dartmouth College. The awards include a $25,000 stipend, a $2,500 supply allowance, and a teaching requirement.

Phone: 603-646-2107

Website: www.dartmouth.edu/~gradstdy/funding/fellowships/

Cross Cultural Institute Fellowships for Research in Japan are one-year, $24,000 awards for master's or doctoral students.

Phone: 319-337-1650

Email: ccigfp@act.org

Five Colleges Fellowship Program for Minority Students provides a residential fellowship for schools in middle Massachusetts. The stipend is $30,000 for one year.

Phone: 413-256-8316

Email: neckert@fivecolleges.edu

Website: www.fivecolleges.edu/academic_programs/academprog_fellowship.html

Ford Foundation Dissertation Fellowships for Minorities provide a one-year, $21,000 stipend for programs in behavioral and social sciences, humanities, engineering, mathematics, physical sciences, life sciences, and education, as well as interdisciplinary programs composed of two or more eligible disciplines.

Phone: 202-334-2872

Email: infofell@nas.edu

Website: www.nationalacademies.org/fellowships/fordiss.html

Fulbright Full Grants support dissertation field research, specifically travel to almost any country (your choice) for an academic year. A stipend, travel, and dependent's allowance are provided, with the amount depending on the host country.

Website: www.iie.org/fulbright/us

Fulbright-Hays Dissertation Fellowships pay more than the Fulbright but are applicable to study in fewer countries. They support 6 to 12 months of research. It is also more difficult to get this award than the Fulbright.

Website: www.ed.gov/programs/iegpsddrap/index.html

Harvard W. E. B. Du Bois Institute Research Fellowships are one-year fellowships to research all aspects of African American life, history, and culture.

Phone: 617-496-6623

Email: du_bois@fas.harvard.edu

Website: www.fas.harvard.edu/~du_bois/

Intercollegiate Studies Institute Western Civilization Fellowships support the study of the institutions, values, and history of the West. The stipend is $20,000 for one year.

Phone: 800-526-7022

Email: awards@isi.org

Website: www.isi.org/programs/fellowships/western_civilization.html

Japan Foundation Doctoral Fellowships support humanities and social science research in Japan. The fellowship includes a stipend, travel, and benefits.

Phone: 212-489-0299

Email: info@jfny.org

Website: www.jfny.org/jfny/applications.html

Kosciuszko Foundation Research Grants in Poland include a stipend, housing, and tuition scholarship to study in Poland.

Phone: 212-734-2130

Email: addy@thekf.org

Website: www.kosciuszkofoundation.org/EDScholarships_PL_Research.html

Matsushita International Foundation Research Grants supports research that develops world culture and peace.

Email: grants@gg.jp.panasonic.com, ajisuka@gg.jp.panasonic.com

The National Foundation for Jewish Culture provides a one-year doctoral dissertation grant of up to $10,000 to study Jewish culture.

Phone: 212-629-0500

Email: Grants@JewishCulture.org

Website: www.jewishculture.org

Social Science Research Council (SSRC) Eastern Europe Fellowships offer a $17,000 stipend and a research allowance for students in the social sciences or humanities.

Phone: 212-377-2700

Email: dheiland@acls.org

Website: www.ssrc.org

Truman Library Fellowships are one-year, nonresidential fellowships for students to write their dissertations. The stipend is $16,000.

Phone: 816-833-0425

Email: lisa.sullivan@truman.nara.gov

Website: www.trumanlibrary.org/grants

University of California—Santa Barbara Women's Studies Dissertation Fellowships support research in the intersections of race, class, gender, sexuality, and cultural difference. The one-year stipend is $20,000.

Phone: 805-893-4330

Email: rondilla@alishaw.ucsb.edu

Williams College Bolin Fellowships for Minority Graduate Students are residential fellowships that pay $30,500 in salary and a $4,000 research allowance, but they require teaching.

Website: www.williams.edu/admin/deanfac/bolin.html

Fellowships in Science and Engineering

Why apply if you have funding from your advisor? Because it demonstrates to job search committees that you can sell your ideas in a competitive market. And extra money never hurts.

American Heart Association Affiliate Pre-doctoral Fellowships help biologists and biochemists initiate careers in cardiovascular or stroke research. The two-year fellowships include a stipend of about $20,000 (the actual amount depends on the regional affiliation that makes the award) per year. It's renewable for a second year.

Email: affil@heart.org

American Lung Association Lung Health Dissertation Grants support doctoral students in the fields of science related to lung disease for up to three years, with a $21,000 annual stipend.

Phone: 1-800-LUNGUSA

Website: www.lungusa.org

Smithsonian Marine Station Fellowships are residential awards for 3 to 24 months that include a $17,000 to $30,000 stipend (depending on whether you are pre- or post-doctoral) and a travel allowance.

Website: www.sms.si.edu/fellowships.htm

Smithsonian Astrophysical Observatory Pre-Doctoral Fellowship Program supports dissertation research on-site. The stipend is about $24,600 per year, renewable for up to three years.

Phone: 617-495-7103

Email: predoc@cfa.harvard.edu

Website: http://cfa-www.harvard.edu/predoc

Research Fellowships in the Humanities

Albright (W.F.) Institute of Archaeological Research Samuel H. Kress Fellowships are for dissertation research on-site in architecture, art history, and archaeology. The student must be a North American citizen studying at an American university. Awards range from $9,000 for six months to $22,500 per year for two years.

Phone: 919-962-3928 (Dr. Jodi Magness)

Email: magness@email.unc.edu

Website: www.wfalbright.org/fellowship.html

American Academy in Rome—Rome Prize Fellowships in Classical Studies are pre- and post-doctoral fellowships in classical studies and archaeology, history of art, and post-classical humanistic/modern Italian studies. They are for a 6- to 24-month period and carry a stipend of up to $15,570 per year. Applicants must be U.S. citizens and have completed all graduate requirements but the dissertation.

Phone: 212-751-7200

Email: info@aarome.org

Website: www.aarome.org

American Institute of Architects AIA/AHA Graduate Fellowship in Health Facilities Planning and Design's goals are to increase the awareness of architecture students in the special needs and nature of health-care facilities. It includes a one-year stipend of up to $13,500, which is renewable for one additional year. You must be a Canadian, Mexican, or U.S. citizen or permanent resident.

Phone: 202-626-7366

Email: jberry@aia.org

Website: www.aia.org/pia/health/gradfell.asp

American Meteorological Society (AMS) Graduate Fellowship in the History of Science is a one-year fellowship to be awarded to a student wishing to complete a dissertation on the history of atmospheric or related oceanic or hydraulic sciences. The stipend award is worth $15,000.

Phone: 617-227-2426 ext. 246

Email: dfernand@ametsoc.org *or* armstrong@ametsoc.org

The American School of Classical Studies at Athens offers an academic-year fellowship with a $15,500 to $25,000 stipend awarded to study human skeletal remains from archaeological contexts in Greece. It is available to scholars with a PhD or graduate students who have completed all but the dissertation.

Email: ascsa@ascsa.edu.gr

Archaeological Institute of America Olivia James Traveling Fellowship is a one-year fellowship for travel and study in mainland Greece, the Aegean Islands, Sicily, Southern Italy, Asia Minor, and Mesopotamia. It is primarily for students of the classics, sculpture, architecture, archaeology, and history. The stipend award is $22,000. You must be a U.S. citizen or permanent resident; post-doctoral students should have received the PhD within the past five years.

Phone: 617-353-8705

Email: egilgan@aia.bu.edu

The Fund for Theological Education, Inc., Dissertation Fellowships for African Americans are one-year awards for African American PhD students at the final writing stage of their graduate work in religious or theological studies. You must be a U.S. citizen. The stipend award is $15,000.

Phone: 404-727-1450

Email: sfluker@thefund.org

Website: www.thefund.org/programs/fellowships/dissertation/index.html

Getty Research Institute for the History of Art, Architecture, and the Humanities, Scholars and Seminars Program Fellowships are for scholars working on projects related to a specific theme. This multiyear dissertation fellowship includes a stipend, an office at the Getty Institute in Los Angeles, and housing. Pre-doctoral students must have completed all but the dissertation.

Phone: 310-440-7374

Email: researchgrants@getty.edu

Website: www.getty.edu/grants/research/scholars/pre_post_fellows.html

The Phi Beta Kappa Society Mary Isabel Sibley Fellowship for Greek Studies is awarded for original research in Greek or French language, literature, history, or archaeology (odd-numbered years), or French language and literature (even-numbered years). It includes a stipend award of $20,000. The candidate must be an unmarried woman between 25 and 35; pre-doctoral students must have completed all but the dissertation.

Phone: 202-265-3808

Email: sbeasley@pbk.org

Website: www.pbk.org/scholarships/sibley.htm

The University of Pennsylvania Philadelphia McNeil Center for Early American Studies Postdoctoral and Dissertation Fellowships Program provides $16,000 to support dissertation research and writing in any aspect of American studies, with a primary focus on the political, social, economic, or cultural development of the North American and the Atlantic region up to 1850.

Phone: 215-898-9251

Website: www.mceas.org/dissertationfellowships.htm

The University of Virginia Carter G. Woodson Institute for Afro-American and African Studies Fellowship Program awards two-year graduate or one-year postdoctoral dissertation fellowships designed to facilitate the completion of dissertations or manuscripts in African American and African studies and related fields. The graduate award is worth $15,000 annually. The candidate must be a U.S. citizen or permanent resident.

Phone: 434-924-3109

Email: woodson@gwis.virginia.edu

Website: www.virginia.edu/woodson/programs/application.html

Woodrow Wilson National Fellowship Foundation Charlotte W. Newcombe Doctoral Dissertation Fellowships encourage original and significant study of ethical or religious values in all fields of the humanities and social sciences. The stipend award is $17,500.

Phone: 609-452-7007

Email: charlotte@woodrow.org

Website: www.woodrow.org

Woodrow Wilson National Fellowship Foundation Andrew W. Mellon Fellowships in Humanistic Studies help exceptionally promising students prepare for careers of teaching and scholarship in humanistic studies. The stipend award is $17,550. The candidate must be a college graduate or have a terminal MA (i.e., there is not a PhD offered in his or her discipline).

Phone: 800-899-9963 ext. 127

Email: mellon@woodrow.org

Website: www.woodrow.org/mellon

Yale University Pew Program in Religion and American History Dissertation Fellowships stimulate and sustain scholarship in religion and American history between 1600 and 1980. The stipend award is $17,000 plus allowances.

Phone: 203-432-5341

Email: cral@yale.edu

Research Fellowships in the Social Sciences

American Council of Learned Societies (ACLS) Dissertation Fellowships in East European Studies support Eastern Europe–related dissertation research or writing to be undertaken outside Eastern Europe. They include a stipend award of up to $17,000. Candidates must be U.S. citizens or permanent residents.

Phone: 212-697-1505

Website: www.acls.org

American Psychological Association Minority Fellowship Program provides multiyear support in mental health and substance abuse services, mental health research, and HIV/AIDS research. You must be a U.S. citizen and member of an underrepresented ethnic group enrolled in a PhD program. The award includes a travel stipend plus $12,000 per year.

Phone: 202-336-6127

Email: mfp@apa.org

Website: www.apa.org/mfp

Berlin Program for Advanced German and European Studies provides 10- to 12-month, residential dissertation fellowships for research at the Free University of Berlin. They encourage comparative and interdisciplinary study of the economic, political, and social aspects of modern and contemporary German and European affairs. Candidates must be U.S. or Canadian citizens or permanent residents; pre-doctoral students must have passed their oral comprehensive exams.

Email: bprogram@zedat.fu-berlin.de

Website: http://userpage.fu-berlin.de/~bprogram/

The Harry Frank Guggenheim Foundation Dissertation Fellowship is a one-year dissertation fellowship for research on the causes, manifestations, and control of violence, aggression, and dominance. Candidates must be writing their dissertations. The stipend award is $15,000.

Phone: 212-644-4907

Website: http://hfg.org

The Harvard Academy for International and Area Studies Academy Scholars Program supports social scientists in area studies, focusing especially on the non-Western areas of the world. Pre-doctoral scholars receive a stipend award of $25,000.

Phone: 617-495-2137

Email: bbaiter@cfia.harvard.edu

Website: www.wcfia.harvard.edu/academy

National Institute of Justice Graduate Research Fellowships provide multiyear support to graduate students whose research focuses on a topic relevant to national criminal justice policy or is directly related to the concerns of operating criminal justice agencies. The fellowship awards stipends of up to $20,000. The candidate must have completed all but the dissertation.

Phone: 202-307-2942

Website: www.ojp.usdoj.gov/nij/funding.htm

National Institutes of Health and National Institute of Mental Health Dissertation Research Grants in Developmental Psychopathology, HIV/AIDS Research, and Mental Health Services Research are 12- to 24-month grants to motivate doctoral candidates to make a commitment to research careers in one of these selected areas of importance to NIMH. You must be a U.S. citizen or permanent resident and must have completed all but the dissertation.

Phone: 301-443-6100

Website: www.nimh.nih.gov

National Security Education Program (NSEP) David L. Boren Graduate Fellowships focus on geographic areas, languages, and fields of study deemed critical to U.S. national security. The maximum stipend award is $10,000 per semester overseas (the maximum is two semesters) or $12,000 per semester at your home institution. You must be a U.S. citizen and must be currently enrolled in or applying to an accredited graduate department in the United States. All applications must include study of a modern language other than English.

Phone: 800-498-9360

Email: nsep@aed.org

Website: http://nsep.aed.org

PricewaterhouseCoopers Research Grants stimulate research and seek to improve the effectiveness of government at the federal, state, local, and international levels. These grants are mainly for social science research. The stipend award is $15,000. Applicants must work in universities, nonprofits, or journalism.

Phone: 703-741-1077

Email: endowment@us.pwcglobal.com

Website: www.endowment.pwcglobal.com/research.asp

Resources for the Future Joseph L. Fisher Dissertation Awards are one-year fellowships supporting dissertation research (in economics or other policy sciences) on issues related to the environment, natural resources, or energy. The stipend award is $12,000.

Phone: 202-328-5000

Website: www.rff.org/rff/About/Fellowships_and_Internships/Fisher/More.cfm

Social Science Research Council (SSRC) Program on the Corporation as a Social Institution is a one-year grant of $10,000 for graduate students working on projects that involve some aspect of corporations, firms, or organizations. Specific themes that are of interest to this initiative include power, culture, varying conceptions of the corporation, networks, intraorganizational structure, governments, and law. Applicants must be advanced to PhD candidacy.

Phone: 212-377-2700

Email: guthrie@ssrc.org

Website: www.ssrc.org

Social Science Research Council (SSRC) Eurasia Program Dissertation Write-Up Fellowships support scholars with a one-year award for writing their dissertations on Eastern Europe, the Russian Empire, or the Soviet Union and its successor states. The stipend is $15,000. You must be a U.S. citizen or permanent resident and finished with course work.

Phone: 212-377-2700

Email: Eurasia@ssrc.org

Website: www.ssrc.org/fellowships/eurasia/dissertation_writeup_fellowships

Social Science Research Council (SSRC) International Dissertation Field Research Fellowship Program (IDRF) are stipends that provide 9 to 12 months of support for social scientists and humanists to conduct dissertation field research in all areas and regions of the world outside the United States. The award is up to $17,000.

Phone: 212-377-2700

Email: idrf@ssrc.org

Website: www.ssrc.org

Spencer Foundation Dissertation Fellowships for Research Related to Education support doctoral candidates in a variety of fields whose dissertations promise to contribute fresh perspectives to the history, theory, or practice of education. The fellowships award stipends of $20,000. Applicants must be candidates for the doctoral degree at graduate schools in the United States.

Phone: 312-274-6526

Email: fellows@spencer.org

Website: www.spencer.org/programs/index.htm

Stanford University Center for International Security and Cooperation Hamburg Fellowships are 9- to 12-month residential awards to promote scholarship focusing on the prevention of deadly conflict, both in the pre-conflict stage and in the implementation phase of peace agreements. Applicants may be from a broad range of disciplines, including law, political science, anthropology, sociology, economics, the natural and physical sciences, medicine, history, and other related fields. The stipend award is $20,000 for a pre-doctoral scholar. Candidates should have completed all but the dissertation.

Phone: 650-723-9626

Email: bplatt@stanford.edu

Website: http://cisac.stanford.edu

Udall (Morris K.) Foundation Dissertation Fellowship Program awards one-year fellowships in the area of environmental public policy and/or environmental conflict resolution. Applicants must be U.S. citizens or permanent residents and must anticipate receiving their doctoral degree at the end of the fellowship year. The stipend award is up to $24,000.

Phone: 520-670-5529

U.S. Department of Housing and Urban Development (HUD) Doctoral Dissertation Research Grant Program provides $15,000 annual stipends to doctoral candidates to complete their research and dissertations on housing and urban development issues. Candidates must have completed all but the dissertation, and can renew the grant for an additional year.

Phone: 800-245-2691

Website: www.oup.org

U.S. Institute of Peace Jennings Randolph Program for International Peace Dissertation Fellowships are one-year awards intended to support the research and writing of dissertations addressing the sources and nature of international conflict and the full range of ways to prevent or end conflict and to sustain peace. Stipends are $17,000. Candidates must have completed all but the dissertation by the commencement of the award.

Phone: 202-457-1700

Website: www.usip.org

Research Grants

The following list consists of awards that are between $1,000 and $10,000. This is not enough money to provide a 12-month stipend and a research allowance. You may be able to eke out a summer on one of these, but the purpose for writing a grant proposal is to pay for extraordinary research expenses such as professional travel, equipment, supplies, databases, etc. There are also special grants to visit specific libraries or learn an exotic language.

Cross-Disciplinary Grants

Lindbergh Foundation Grants are one-year grants to support research that seeks to promote a better balance between the advancement of technology and the preservation of the human/natural environment. The stipend award is up to $10,580 (the cost of building the *Spirit of St. Louis* in 1927).

Phone: 763-576-1596

Email: info@lindberghfoundation.org

Website: www.lindberghfoundation.org

Sigma Delta Epsilon Graduate Women in Science Fellowships are one-year awards for research in all the natural sciences, including physical, environmental, mathematical, computer, life sciences, anthropology, psychology, and statistics. The maximum stipend is $4,000. The candidate must be enrolled as a graduate student and be a member of SDE/GWIS.

Email: kelleyk@ohio.edu

Website: www.gwis.org/grants

Grants in Science and Engineering

American Association of Petroleum Geologists (AAPG) Grants-in-Aid Program issues awards of up to $2,000 for graduate research projects related to earth science aspects of the petroleum industry. The program focuses on support for master's or equivalent degrees.

Email: gia@aapg.org

Website: http://foundation.aapg.org/gia

American Federation for Aging Research (AFAR) Scholarships for Research in the Biology of Aging are $6,000 grants awarded to PhD candidates and medical students for research on any topic related to the biology of aging.

Phone: 212-703-9977

Email: grants@afar.org

Website: www.afar.org

American Geophysical Union Horton Research Grants support research projects in hydrology and water resources by PhD candidates. The stipend amount is unspecified but averages about $10,000.

Phone: 800-966-2481

Website: http://hydrology.agu.org

American Museum of Natural History Theodore Roosevelt Memorial Fund Grants provide modest short-term support for advanced graduate students and post-doctoral researchers who are commencing their careers in paleontology. The Roosevelt Memorial Fund supports research on North American fauna (except birds). The stipend ranges from $200 to $2,000, and the average is $1,400.

Phone: 212-769-5495

Email: grants@amnh.org

Website: http://research.amnh.org/grants

American Society of Heating, Refrigerating, and Air-Conditioning Engineers (ASHRAE), Inc., Grant-in-Aid for Graduate Students is a one-year, nonrenewable award to a full-time graduate student of ASHRAE-related technologies to encourage preparation for service in the industry. Typical expenditures include living expenses, tuition, travel to ASHRAE meetings, experimental equipment, and supplies. Applications must be made by a faculty advisor on the student's behalf. The stipend award is up to $10,000.

Phone: 404-636-8400

Email: mvaughn@ashrae.org

Website: www.ashrae.org

American Water Works Association (AWWA) Holly A. Cornell Scholarships support outstanding female and/or minority students to pursue advanced training in the field of water supply and treatment. The award amount is $5,000. Applicants must be female and/or minority U.S. citizens.

Phone: 303-347-6206

Email: ncole@awwa.org

Website: www.awwa.org

Arthritis Foundation Doctoral Dissertation Awards for Arthritis Health Professionals are multiyear dissertation grants supporting dissertation research in arthritis management and/or comprehensive patient care in rheumatology practice, research, or education. The award amount is $10,000 per year. Candidates must be U.S. citizens or permanent residents and must have membership or eligibility for membership in the relevant professional organization.

Phone: 404-965-7636

Website: www.arthritis.org

Geological Society of America (GSA) Research Grants Program provides partial support of master's and doctoral thesis research. The stipend award averages $1,800. Candidates must be members of the GSA.

Phone: 303-357-1028

Email: awards@geosociety.org

Website: www.geosociety.org/grants/gradgrants.htm

Huyck (Edmund Niles) Preserve, Inc., Graduate and Postgraduate Research Grants support research at the Biological Research Station of the Huyck Preserve (Rensselaerville, New York) in which the natural resources of the preserve are used. Fields of study include ecology, biogeography, taxonomy, behavior, evolution, and systematics. The award amount is up to $2,500.

Phone: 518-797-3440

Website: www.huyckpreserve.org

Illinois-Indiana Sea Grant Program Graduate Fellowship provides multiyear funding to pursue studies related to the southern Lake Michigan region. The stipend is $3,000.

Phone: 217-333-0045

Email: lmorrisn@uiuc.edu

Website: www.iisgcp.org

National Science Foundation Directorate of Biological Sciences Doctoral Dissertation Improvement Grants provide partial support for dissertation research with an ecological, evolutionary, or behavioral focus. The stipend award ranges from $3,000 to $12,000. Applicants must have advanced to PhD candidacy.

Phone: 703-292-8480 (Environmental Biology) or

703-292-7875 (Integrative Biology and Neuoroscience)

Website: www.nsf.gov

Sigma XI Grants-in-Aid of Research support scientific investigation in any field. Stipend awards are generally up to $1,000 (up to $2,500 for astronomy or vision research).

Phone:800-243-6534

Website: www.sigmaxi.org/programs/giar/index.shtml

Social Science Grants

American Educational Research Association (AERA) Dissertation Grants Program aims to stimulate research on U.S. education policy and practice-related issues, with a priority for those involving mathematics and science education using NCES and NSF data sets. The stipend award is $15,000 for one year. Candidates must be U.S. citizens or permanent residents.

Phone: 805-964-5264

Email: jmurdock@aera.net

Website: www.aera.net

Columbia University Council for European Studies Pre-Dissertation Fellowships are three types of summer grants for research in Europe, all of which are restricted to doctoral candidates at member universities. The stipend is $4,000.

Phone: 212-854-4172

Email: ces@columbia.edu

Website: www.columbia.edu/cu/ces

Dirksen Congressional Center Congressional Research Grants Program are one-year renewable grants to research the study of leadership in the U.S. Congress. Sample topics include external and institutional factors that shape and affect the exercise of leadership, resources and techniques used by leaders, and prospects for change or continuity. The grant covers travel, research materials, and research assistance. The stipend is up to $3,500.

Phone: 309-347-7113

Email: fmackaman@pekin.net

Website: www.dirksencenter.org

International Education Research Foundation Research Grants aim to help scholars investigate educational systems of the world and publish and distribute findings exclusively for charitable, scientific, and educational purposes to interested persons and organizations on a nondiscriminatory basis.

Phone: 310-258-9451

Email: grants@ierf.org

Jacobs Foundation Dissertation Grants and Young Investigator Grants in Adolescence and Youth Research support empirical research investigations conducted as dissertation projects. Fields covered include the behavioral, educational, and social sciences in three general areas of interest in research on youth and adolescence: development of life skills and social competence, sensitivity toward nature and the environment, and capability to effectively use modern information technology. The stipend award is up to $5,000.

Phone: +41 1 388 61 23

Email: jf@jacobsfoundation.org

Website: www.jacobsfoundation.org/program/p4.htm

National Science Foundation Minority Graduate Student Travel Awards seek to assist candidates in the selection of a postdoctoral mentor and in the development of an application for an NSF Minority Postdoctoral Research Fellowship. They may also be used to attend professional meetings to meet potential mentors. Proposed research must fall within the program areas of the Directorate for Biological Sciences or the Directorate for Social, Behavioral, and Economic Sciences. The stipend award is up to $3,000. The candidate must be a U.S. citizen who is member of a specified minority group and must be within 18 months of earning a PhD.

Phone: 703-306-1469

Email: ckimsey@nsf.gov

Website: www.nsf.gov

National Science Foundation Science and Technology Studies (STS) Doctoral Dissertation Research Grants are one-year awards focused on improving knowledge of ethical and value dimensions in science, engineering, and technology. The stipend award is $8,000 for work in the United States and $12,000 for work abroad.

Phone: 703-292-8763

Email: rholland@nsf.gov

Website: www.nsf.gov

National Science Foundation Directorate for Social, Behavioral, and Economic Sciences Dissertation Improvement Awards are multiyear grants to improve the quality of dissertation research. They are awarded for data-gathering projects and field research. The stipend award is normally $7,500 or less.

Phone: 703-306-1700

Email: pwhite@nsf.gov

Website: www.nsf.gov

Radcliffe College Murray Research Center Dissertation Awards—Adolescent and Youth Dissertation Awards support research on youth and adolescent development. Proposals focusing on "youth as a resource" or positive attributes and strengths of youth are especially encouraged. Any student currently enrolled in a doctoral program in a relevant field is eligible to apply. The stipend is up to $5,000.

Phone: 617-495-8140

Email: mrc@radcliffe.edu

Website: www.radcliffe.edu/murray/grants/index.htm

Social Science Research Council (SSRC) Grants for Research Collaboration in Conflict Zones are four- to six-month research grants awarded to qualified teams of individuals who currently reside or work in places where there are long-standing, intractable, or widespread violent conflicts. The proposed research should contribute to the generation of new perspectives, knowledge, and data about underlying causes of violent conflicts. The stipend award is up to $10,000.

Phone: 202-732-5572

Email: schuppert@ssrc.org

Website: www.ssrc.org

Social Science Research Council (SSRC)/American Council of Learned Societies (ACLS)/South Africa's National Research Foundation (NRF)/Council for the Development of Social Science Research in Africa (CODESRIA)/African Youth in a Global Age programs offer support to researchers studying globalization and its impact on African youth in local, social, and historical contexts. To the extent possible, proposals should also address the theoretical and practical implications of the research. The stipend is up to $10,000 per year for field research.

Phone: 212-377-2700 ext. 452

Email: africa@ssrc.org

Social Science Research Council (SSRC) Japan Foundation Center for Global Partnership Abe Fellowship Program provides support for 3 to 12 months to scholars investigating policy-relevant topics to build bridges between Japanese and American intellectual and professional communities. The candidate must hold a PhD or terminal degree in his or her field and must be a U.S. or Japanese citizen.

Phone: 212-377-2700

Email: abe@ssrc.org

Website: www.ssrc.org

Society for the Psychological Study of Social Issues (SPSSI) Dalmas A. Taylor Summer Minority Policy Fellowship, a one-summer grant, will provide an opportunity for a graduate student to work on public policy issues in Washington, D.C. The candidate must be a graduate student in good standing and a member of an ethnic minority group who has demonstrated a commitment to a career in psychology or a related field with a focus on ethnic minority issues. The stipend award is $3,000 plus housing and travel funds.

Phone: 202-675-6956

Email: spssi@spssi.org

Website: www.spssi.org/taylor_flyer.pdf

Society for the Psychological Study of Social Issues (SPSSI) Grants-in-Aid Program offers support for scientific research in social problem areas related to the basic interests and goals of SPSSI. Proposals in areas that are not likely to receive funding from traditional sources are especially welcome. Funding of up to $1,000 is available for graduate students if the proposal is accompanied by official university agreement to match the amount requested.

Phone: 202-675-6956

Email: spssi@spssi.org

Website: www.spssi.org/giaflyer.pdf

Tinker Foundation Tinker Field Research Grants are for one year, with the possibility of two one-year extensions. They are restricted to travel costs of graduate students conducting pre-dissertation research in Spain, Portugal, and the Spanish- and Portuguese-speaking countries of Latin America. The stipend amounts are $10,000 or $15,000, which must be matched by university or other sources.

Phone: 212-421-6858

Email: tinker@tinker.org

U.S. Department of State Hubert H. Humphrey Doctoral Fellowships support dissertation research in a variety of disciplines designed to contribute to a better understanding of current and future arms control, nonproliferation, and disarmament issues. Candidates must be U.S. citizens or permanent residents and must have completed all but the dissertation. The stipend award is $8,000. The state will also pay up to $6,000 in applicable tuition and fees to the institution in which the fellow is enrolled.

Phone: 202-647-4153

Website: www.state.gov/www/global/arms/fellows.html

Grants in the Humanities

Albright (W.F.) Institute of Archaeological Research George A. Barton Fellowship is a five-month grant open to seminarians, pre-doctoral students, and recent PhD recipients specializing in Near Eastern archaeology, geography, history, and biblical studies. The stipend is $2,950; recipients also receive $4,050 for room and board.

Phone: 216-397-4705

Email: spencer@jcu.edu

Website: www.aiar.org

American Historical Association (AHA) Bernadotte Schmitt Grants are for research in the history of Europe, Asia, and Africa. They may be used for travel to a library or archive for microfilms, photographs, photocopying, etc. Preference is given to PhD candidates and junior scholars. The stipend award is up to $1,000.

Phone: 202-544-2422

Email: aha@theaha.org

Website: www.theaha.org

American Historical Association (AHA) Albert J. Beveridge Grant for Research in the History of the Western Hemisphere is an award of up to $1,000 for research in the history of the Western Hemisphere. It may be used for travel to a library or archive for microfilms, photographs, photocopying, etc. Preference is given to PhD candidates and junior scholars. Candidates must be U.S. citizens and members of the AHA.

Phone: 202-544-2422

Email: aha@theaha.org

Website: www.theaha.org

American Historical Association (AHA) Littleton-Griswold Research Grant supports research in American legal history and the field of law and society. It may be used for travel to a library or archive for microfilms, photographs, photocopying, etc. Preference is given to PhD candidates and junior scholars. Candidates must be U.S. citizens and members of the AHA.

Phone: 202-544-2422

Email: aha@theaha.org

Website: www.theaha.org

American Numismatic Society Donald Groves Fund promotes publication in the field of early American numismatics involving material dating no later than 1800. Funding is available for travel and other expenses in association with research as well as for publication costs.

Phone: 212-234-3130

Email: info@amnumsoc.org

Website: www.amnumsoc.org

The American Research Center in Egypt (ARCE)/Samuel H. Kress Foundation Kress Fellowship in Egyptian Art and Architecture is an annual prize given to a pre-doctoral candidate of any nationality. The stipend is $12,800, plus round-trip airfare to Egypt.

Phone: 404-712-9854

Email: arce@emory.edu

Website: www.arce.org

British Institute in Eastern Africa (BIEA) Research Grants assist scholars undertaking original research in Eastern Africa in any field of the humanities and social sciences with some emphasis on archaeology, African history, anthropology, and related subjects. Minor research grant proposals cannot exceed £1,000.

Email: pjlane@insightkenya.com

Website: www.britac.ac.uk

DAAD (German Academic Exchange Service) Leo Baeck Institute Grants assist doctoral students or recent PhDs in research on the social, communal, and intellectual history of German-speaking Jewry. Funds are available for research in Germany or New York. The stipend is worth about EUR 795–EUR 975.

Phone: 212-744-6400

Email: lbaeck@lbi.cjh.org

Website: www.daad.org

Early American Industries Association, Inc., Grants-in-Aid are awards of up to $2,000 to assist graduate students and scholars with research leading to publication, exhibitions, or audiovisual materials that relate to the study of early American industries and the discovery of obsolete tools used in early America, up to 1900. The grant may be used only specifically for research and not for overhead expenses or salary of the recipient.

Phone: 302-652-7297

Lemmermann Foundation Scholarship Awards are short-term (two to six months) scholarships for university students who need to study in Rome to carry out research and prepare their theses in the classics or humanities. Topics should concern Rome and Roman culture from the pre-Roman period to the present day.

Phone: +39 06 324 30 23

Email: lemmermann@mail.nexus.it

Website: http://lemmermann.nexus.it/lemmermann

Hagley Museum and Library Hagley-Winterthur Fellowships provide short-term (one to six months) support with a stipend award of up to $1,400 per month. The award gives access to the Winterthur Museum and Gardens and the Hagley Museum and Library for scholars interested in the historical and cultural relationships between economic life and the arts, including design, architecture, crafts, and the fine arts.

Phone: 302-658-2400

Website: www.hagley.lib.de.us/grants.html

Memorial Foundation for Jewish Culture International Fellowships in Jewish Studies are awarded for one academic year to assist well-qualified individuals in carrying out an independent scholarly, literary, or art project, in a field of Jewish specialization, that makes a significant contribution to the understanding, preservation, enhancement, or transmission of Jewish culture. The stipend award varies in accordance with the cost of living in the country in which the fellowship recipient resides and ranges up to $7,500 per year.

Phone: 212-425-6606

National Association of Dealers in Antiques Scholarship Fund offers support to graduate students seeking an advanced degree in museum studies with a focus on object conservation, historic preservation with object emphasis, or a cognate program. The stipend award is up to $3,000.

Phone: 800-486-5372

Email: antiques@nadaweb.org

National Research Council (NRC) Travel and Research Grants—Eastern Europe are short-term funds available for graduate students and post-docs working on governance in post-communist societies in East Central Europe or in the former Soviet Union. Areas of interest are science and democratization, organized crime, terrorism, and proliferation of weapons of mass destruction.

Phone: 202-334-2658

Email: sdeets@nas.edu

Organization of American Historians (OAH) Horace Samuel & Marion Galbraith Merrill Travel Grants in Twentieth Century American Political History promote access of younger scholars to the Washington, D.C., region's rich primary source collections in late-nineteenth- and twentieth-century American political history. The grants also provide the opportunity for scholars to interview former and current public figures residing in the metropolitan Washington area. Stipends ranging from $500 to $3,000 are offered to underwrite travel and lodging expenses for members of the OAH who are working toward completion of a dissertation or first book.

Website: www.oah.org/activities/awards/merrill/index.html

Organization of American Historians (OAH)/National Park Service Jamestown Scholars Dissertation Fellowships are stipend awards of $5,000 made to support PhD research that contributes to understanding the development and legacy of seventeenth-century Jamestown, the first permanent English colony in North America, where diverse peoples from three continents came together. The competition is open to U.S. graduate students pursuing PhDs in history, American studies, and related fields.

Phone: 812-855-9852

Email: jamestown@oah.org

Website: www.oah.org/activities/awards/jamestown/index.html

The Program for Cultural Cooperation offers short-term (up to three months) support for scholars in the United States who wish to undertake or complete research projects in Spain. The stipend award covers 50 percent of total costs, up to $2,000 per month.

Phone: 612-625-9888

Email: spain@admu.edu.ph

The Sinfonia Foundation Research Assistance Grants in Music are stipends of up to $1,000 for scholarly research in music. The subject of the research must be related to American music or to music in America.

Phone: 800-473-2649

Email: lyrecrest@sinfonia.org

Website: www.sinfoniafoundation.org/research.html

U.S. Army Center of Military History Dissertation Fellowships are one-year grants of $8,000 to support preparation of dissertations on the history of war on land. Recipients must visit the Center at the beginning and end of the fellowship period.

Phone: 202-685-2094

Email: edgar.raines@hqda.army.mil

Website: www.army.mil/cmh-pg

Yale Center for British Art Paul Mellon Junior Fellowships are short-term (three months) grants in the U.K. (based at the Paul Mellon Centre in London) or the U.S. (based at the Yale Center for British Art in New Haven) and one offered to scholars already engaged in doctoral research. The award includes a stipend of £1,500 or $1,500 and round-trip airfare. Candidates must be enrolled in a graduate program at an American university (for study in the U.K.) or at a non-American university (for study in the U.S.).

Phone: 44 20 7580 0311

Email: grants@paul-mellon-centre.ac.uk

Humanities and Social Sciences Grants

American Institute of Indian Studies Junior Research Fellowships are available to doctoral candidates at U.S. colleges or universities in all fields of study. Junior fellowships are specifically designed to enable doctoral candidates to pursue their dissertation research in India.

Phone: 773-702-8638

Email: aiis@uchicago.edu

Website: http://humanities.uchicago.edu/orgs/aiis

The American Research Center in Egypt (ARCE)/U.S. State Department Bureau of Educational and Cultural Affairs Pre-Doctoral and Post-doctoral Fellowships are short-term (3 to 12 months) grants that include a monthly stipend commensurate with academic status and number of accompanying dependents, plus round-trip air transportation for recipients only.

Phone: 404-712-9854

Email: arce@emory.edu

Website: www.arce.org

Canadian Studies Graduate Student Fellowship Program provides grants for up to nine months to conduct doctoral research in Canada. The dissertation must be related in substantial part to the study of Canada, Canada/U.S. relations, or Canada/North America relations. The stipend award is up to U.S. $8,000. Candidates must be U.S. citizens or permanent residents and must have completed all but the dissertation.

Phone: 202-682-7717

Email: danial.abele@dfait-maeci.gc.ca

Website: www.canadianembassy.org

DAAD (German Academic Exchange Service) German Studies Research Grants are awarded to graduate students nominated by their department/program chairs. The grants are tenable for short-term research in either North America or Germany. The program is designed to encourage research and promote the study of cultural, political, historical, economic, and social aspects of modern and contemporary German affairs from an inter- and multidisciplinary perspective. The stipend award is between $1,500 and $3,000.

Phone: 212-758-3223

Email: daadny@daad.org

Website: www.daad.org

Georgetown University Institute of Turkish Studies—Pre-dissertation Research and Training Grants are reserved for those who have completed at least one year of modern Turkish (exceptions may be made for those applying from institutions where Turkish is not taught). These grants are for summer travel to Turkey for language study and/or research. They are not intended for students currently engaged in dissertation research or writing. The stipend award is between $1,000 and $2,000. The candidate must be a U.S. citizen or permanent resident and must be a graduate student in any field of the social sciences or humanities.

Phone: 202-687-0295

Email: sayaris@gunet.georgetown.edu

Website: www.turkishstudies.org

International Research and Exchanges Board (IREX) Individual Advanced Research Opportunities are short-term (2 to 12 months) grants to support research projects in Central and Eastern Europe, Mongolia, or Eurasia. Applicants are encouraged to apply for U.S. Department of Education Fulbright-Hays Grants. The stipend varies but includes travel plus other allowances. Candidates must be U.S. citizens or permanent residents; pre-doctoral students must have completed all but the dissertation.

Phone: 202-628-8188

Email: irex@irex.org

Website: www.irex.org

Rockefeller Archive Center Research Grant Program provides funds to scholars engaged in projects based substantially on the holdings of the Center. The size of the grant depends on travel, temporary lodging, and research expenses. The stipend award is up to $3,000 or $4,000 for those coming from outside North America.

Phone: 914-631-6017

Email: archive@rockefeller.edu

Website: www.rockefeller.edu/archive.ctr

Woodrow Wilson National Fellowship Foundation Johnson & Johnson Dissertation Grants in Women & Children's Health are intended to encourage original and significant research on issues related to women and children's health. The stipend award is $6,000.

Phone: 609-452-7007

Email: charlotte@woodrow.org

Website: www.woodrow.org

Woodrow Wilson National Fellowship Foundation Woodrow Wilson Dissertation Grants in Women's Studies are for expenses connected with dissertation research on women's role in society, women in history, psychology of women, and women as seen in literature and art. The stipend award is $3,000.

Phone: 609-452-7007

Email: charlotte@woodrow.org

Website: www.woodrow.org

Tips on Writing Grant and Fellowship Applications

Fellowships that fund the early part of your graduate career generally rely more on your undergraduate record and GRE scores than on an elaborate research plan. This section deals mostly with dissertation grants and fellowships. You can apply for these only after you have a dissertation topic in hand.

Why write a grant or fellowship application? The most obvious answer is because your research probably requires money for travel, equipment, supplies, and uninterrupted time to collect data and write. But even if you don't need that much money, there are several reasons for going through the process. First, it gives you experience in a professional activity that is an integral part of any researcher's career. Second, it tells future faculty search committees that your research ideas are marketable. Third, success is self-perpetuating. The mere fact that you were funded once will make you more competitive for the next fellowship or grant.

It is important to remember that a grant or a fellowship application is a sales document. You are selling your credentials and your ideas to a selection committee whose members have to read far more applications than there is money to hand out. If you cannot quickly convey a research question in a clear, forceful, and enthusiastic manner, these committee members will not remember you or your idea. As a graduate student, the task of developing a dissertation grant application is even more difficult because the time between knowing what you want to do and graduation is so short.

Therefore, **plan a year or two ahead**. Many research fellowship applications are written a year before the funding kicks in. This means that the research idea has to be developed, the methodology learned, researchers who can help you contacted, and the potential sources of funding identified *at least* 14 months before you actually get the money to do the work.

Where do you **develop the research idea**? You are in a university. Ideas will be coming at you from all sides. You have classes to sit in, lectures to prepare, papers to read, seminars and discussion groups to attend, written and oral comprehensive examinations to pass, and the occasional coffee and conversation with classmates and faculty. The trick is to capture these ideas and adapt them to your own subdiscipline. Write down the ideas that come to you; look back over the list frequently to discard the bad and the trite and to add more substance to the potentially good, unanswered questions. Eliminate topics that are not central to your discipline or that are not novel. Your graduate advisor and a little of your own research will help you there. Consider comparative analysis or interdisciplinary topics, which are rich in questions but require becoming an expert in two topics. (It also makes you marketable in two disciplines.) A good research question has an answer that is important. A good dissertation question, however, must be answered in about two to four years, so a large, important question may have to be broken down into feasible (but just as valid) parts. It is also best to design a research question where either "yes" or "no" answers are interesting answers.

For instance, you decide to find a cure for the common cold for your dissertation topic. Granted, this is an important question but not likely to be solved quickly or it would have already been done by a drug company. Furthermore, your inability to come up with a cure means that you have nothing to say in your dissertation. If, however, you ask if a particular strain of cold virus enters the cultured cells of the upper respiratory tract through a certain set of receptors, you have a more valid and feasible question that leads ultimately to the more important question.

How do you **obtain the necessary credentials**? Once you have a general idea where your research is going, you need to determine what skills are necessary to do the research. Do you need one or more languages? Will statistics be necessary to prove your point? Will you be accessing a database or other unfamiliar software? Will certain technical skills and equipment be needed to run experiments? Is the library adequate? Make a list of what you need. Cross off those skills that you can prove you have mastered (in transcripts, examinations, research presentations, and publications). Figure out what local resources are available to help you learn the necessary new techniques or who might do things for you (not always a good idea when you are in training). If there are important items left on the list, ask your graduate advisor who outside the university might provide the help. If your advisor doesn't have any suggestions, you will have to look up publications in which the method you need was used and find out where it was done. It is not necessary that you have everything mastered by the time you write the proposal. After all, you will have a year before you get funded anyway. However, you will have to prove to the award committee that you will have all of the critical pieces in place by the time the funding becomes available.

Once you have a general idea of what you plan to do and what you will need to do it, it is time to **find potential funding sources**. We have discussed this topic and listed some of the more common fellowship offerings earlier in this chapter. Once you get a list of possible funding sources, you should go to the Internet to see if the sponsor has a website that contains eligibility requirements, deadlines, and the number and amount of the awards. If there is any question that you or your project will not be welcomed, contact the agency and ask. Otherwise you may be wasting a lot of time. Ask for an application and read it carefully. Make sure that you follow the directions exactly, especially the application deadline. Remember that the easiest way to reduce the number of applications is to cull all those applicants who didn't follow instructions or were otherwise ineligible. Don't ever assume that your qualifications and proposal are so magnificent that no one will notice that you haven't passed your oral comprehensive examination yet or that the proposal is seven pages too long or that it arrived a week late. No reviewer will ever see the application.

Now you are ready to sit down and **write the proposal**. Your goal is to state clearly what the research question is and why the answer is important. You have to make this a compelling case in the first page (preferably the first paragraph) of the proposal. Later you have to prove that you are a person qualified to do this research and that the plan and methods you will use are valid and feasible.

Many sponsors will define the length and organization of the proposal. Do not deviate from the directions. If there are no directions, we suggest that you begin with enough background to understand the research question followed quickly by a clear and succinct statement of purpose. Follow up with a section on the significance of your research. Do not assume that everyone will intuitively understand the significance. The second half of the proposal should contain preliminary results from pilot studies or short field trips (if there are any) and the methods that you propose to use to answer the research question. The more specific you can be concerning methodology without becoming tediously technical, the better. Instead of saying that you will be doing archival research in Paris, tell the reviewers which archives, which important documents you discovered in a previous field trip, the method for gaining access to the archives, and the courses you have taken to assist you in the translation of these documents. Listing every single document is technically tedious. Also, instead of saying that you will be taking courses at the university, tell the reviewers which courses, who will be teaching those courses, and who has invited you to participate in the classes. Giving course numbers and times is overkill. Finally, make sure that your project is manageable within the time frame of the grant or fellowship.

With regard to writing style, always keep in mind that reviewers have a stack of proposals in front of them and not much time to stop and wonder what the hell you just wrote. Therefore, keep most of your sentences short and direct, choose active over passive voice, and avoid jargon. Jargon is disciplinary shorthand and is useful for those in the subdiscipline. Award committees, however, may be interdisciplinary in nature and unfamiliar with your language. Use positive language such as "will" and "can" instead of "may" or "might." The former verbs convey confidence.

With regard to appearance, remember that a well-conceived layout will emphasize your important points. White space and boldface are important organizers. Don't cram more information into the narrative by reducing the margins or decreasing the font size. Use spelling and grammar checkers and be neat. Put the proposal down for a week and then proofread it. Get your advisor and other members of the dissertation committee to read the proposal. They will tell you whether your objective is clearly stated and the research plan is logically arranged. Ask researchers from outside the field. They will circle undefined terms and jargon and tell you if you made a compelling case for doing the project.

Just remember that a reviewer will not appreciate your idea if it is presented poorly. The assumption is that the quality of the proposal will mirror the quality of the research and the final product. You do not want to spend another year in graduate school revising the application.

Can you submit the same idea to more than one funding agency? Absolutely! Once the first proposal is written, it is a much smaller project to adapt it to fit a different format. What is unethical is accepting two awards to accomplish the same project without first discussing the matter with both funding agencies. If neither agency is fully funding the project, you have a case to ask for both. Maybe the two agencies will negotiate with each other to see who will pay. It's a nice problem to have, but don't get sneaky and greedy or you will end up ruining your reputation.

Employer-Financed Opportunities

On-the-job training is the best way for part-time students to get support for going to graduate school. It is also the best deal for students who are anchored to a specific geographical area for personal reasons. The National Center for Education Statistics (NCES) reported that a quarter of graduate students received on average $3,550 in support from their employers in the 1999–2000 academic year. Employers, however, are not altruistic in their support. They will expect the advanced degree to enhance your performance and/or make you eligible for a different job within the company. They may also expect you to stay on for a number of years after you get the degree. Be sure that you understand all aspects of the contract between you and your employer before you sign on.

The military has several educational opportunities for active duty personnel, even rare money for degrees in law and the health professions. For instance, the U.S. Air Force has the Funded Legal Education Program (FLEP), which provides $6,000 in tuition and maintains your base pay. See www.jaguaf.hq.af.mil for more information. The Air Force health professions scholarship is even more lucrative, paying full tuition, books, and fees and offering a stipend. Call 800-531-5800. The U.S. Army has advanced training for active duty personnel in occupational therapy, physical therapy, pharmacology, clinical psychology, and dietetics as well as a physician's assistant program. If the base educational benefits officer can't help you, call the local recruiter, or call 800-USA-ARMY. Active duty personnel of all services may also try for the health professions scholarships listed in the next section. Of course, the Montgomery GI bill helps keep the wolves at bay when you head off for graduate school.

Another government agency, the Peace Corps, offers fellowships to its returning volunteers. The Peace Corps Fellows/USA graduate fellowship program provides funding to earn certification, master's degrees, or doctorates in a wide variety of disciplines, including education. Visit www.peacecorps.gov/gradschool for more information. Americorps programs (VISTA, Americorps National Civilian Community Corps) provide a $4,725 educational allowance for its volunteers as well. Visit www.americorps.org or call 800-942-2677.

The university is probably the employer that will give you the widest latitude in selection of disciplines with the lowest level of commitment on your part. Many schools have tuition scholarships or waivers for a few credits per semester. It may take you awhile to get the degree, but the time of transit between job and school will be eliminated, and the price will be right. Just remember that there are often two tracks, nondegree- and degree-seeking. You must be admitted to the department as a graduate student in order to put the credits toward your degree, and you may not be able to transfer in credits that you earned in a nondegree status.

OTHER GOVERNMENT FUNDING SOURCES

The U.S. military has two different ways to pay for your advanced degree in a health profession: scholarships to a school of your choice or admission to its own medical school. The Uniformed Services University of the Health Sciences, in Bethesda, Maryland, offers degrees in medicine and nursing. Its mission is to train health professionals dedicated to career service in the Department of Defense or the U.S. Public Health Service. In other words, for a free medical education you will be expected to put in time in uniform. Visit www.usuhs.mil for more details.

As for scholarships to "civilian" medical schools, you have the Armed Forces Health Professions Scholarship Program. For instance, the Army offers up to three years of support toward a degree in nursing, medicine, dentistry, optometry, or veterinary medicine. Tuition, books, supplies, and fees are covered, and a $1,100 per month stipend is provided. The Navy and Air Force have similar programs. Call your local ROTC unit or recruiter for more information.

The U.S. Public Health Service also has scholarships paying full tuition, books, fees, and a stipend. You must, however, enter a primary care residency and serve in an inner city or rural setting for as many years as you receive the scholarship. Visit http://bphc.hrsa.gov/nhsc for more information. State governments may also have similar deals.

Law students are also eligible for Reserve Officer Training Corps (ROTC) scholarships and then a Judge Advocate General (JAG) job upon graduation. Check each of your school's ROTC units for more details or each service's JAG website.

In order to qualify for these programs, you must be a U.S. citizen and be qualified for commissioning as a military officer. The obvious advantage to these military/public health service scholarships is that you leave professional school well fed and debt-free. You also have a guaranteed job upon graduation that pays as well or better than what most novice lawyers or physicians get. The disadvantages include a time-in-service *requirement* for every year of scholarship received. Furthermore, you may be ordered to a post in the middle of a swamp and be limited in your on-the-job experience.

A few universities receive training grants from various agencies of the federal government. For instance, the Department of Education's **McNair Program** supports graduate students who are the first in their families to attend college. This is a university-wide program and may be overlooked by your academic department, so be sure to ask the director of graduate studies whether the program exists on your campus. Department-specific funding possibilities are provided by the National Institutes of Health (**NIH Training Grants** in biology, chemistry, psychology, etc.), the National Science Foundation (**NSF IGERT and VIGRE grants** in math, engineering, and science), and the Department of

Education (**GAANNP**). You are invited by the faculty who applied for these grants to join as a trainee, so you will have to be committed to a discipline to have a chance. The Peace Corps offers the **Master's International Program** at participating institutions, which requires 27 months' service upon graduation. See www.peacecorps.gov for details.

Finally, do not overlook university, state, and federal government programs that promote certain agendas. For instance, the Alliance for Catholic Education at the University of Notre Dame pays for your master's in education and certification while you teach. Get to an online search engine, and plug in your discipline of interest and the state or school of choice.

Assessing Multiple Offers and Negotiating

If you receive multiple aid offers from different graduate programs that include a stipend and tuition scholarship, there are objective and subjective ways to help you make a decision.

The objective criteria include the net worth of the offer and the reputation of the department. You need to subtract the student fees (e.g., health center, student activity, technology) and medical insurance costs that you are expected to pay. Then you should determine whether you are classified as a student or as an employee. If you are considered an employee, FICA taxes will be irretrievably withheld, union dues may be charged, and your tuition scholarship may be considered as taxable income. Next, determine how much summer stipend money is available and the percentage of full-time students who are funded in the summer. Finally, go to the library to determine what the cost of living index is for the school's geographical area. Once you have all of these data points, you will know the net worth of the financial package in the first year.

At this point you ought to ask how many years of support are guaranteed, assuming satisfactory academic progress, and the time-to-degree in your discipline for full-time students. This will tell you how much the degree will cost over time and how much you will have to take out of savings or loans to make ends meet. A worksheet on page 166 will help you make the calculations. If the net stipends are within $1,000 of each other, there is no financial reason for choosing one department over another.

More important than the money is the reputation of the department that you are considering. A highly regarded department will have faculty doing cutting-edge research. You are more likely to pick an advisor who is well placed in the field to help you get a job upon graduation. You will also be in a more highly selected peer group that will both challenge you and help you succeed. If you have already hooked up with a highly regarded faculty researcher, then the overall reputation of the department and school is not as important.

The most important consideration is subjective, and to appraise it, you will have to visit the departments that show interest in you. Many schools have recruiting weekends and will even pay for your trip. Whether it is an official paid trip or an unofficial visit, you ought to go to the department, talk to the director of graduate studies, meet faculty who are doing research that interests you, and interview graduate students in the department. Finally, check out the resources (e.g., the library and research laboratories) that you will need to do your research. Remember that departments are evaluating you at the same time, so be appropriately impressed and appreciative. Expect big departments and big schools to be more impersonal and urban campuses to be grittier.

On your way home from these visits, grade the students, the faculty, and the facilities and list what turned you on and what turned you off. Compare your experiences at one school to those at the other schools you're considering. At the end of the process, pick the school with which you feel the most comfortable, a place that is challenging without being intimidating and has people whom you can work with and for. As Barbara Lovitts explains, attrition happens not because you washed out academically but because you did not fit into the culture.

Educational Loans

The Application and Delivery Process

Applying for educational loans has become easier than ever through advances in technology and because of competitive dynamics within the student loan industry to simplify and standardize the entire process. What had required the completion of many forms and a lengthy processing cycle has now become an online, almost instantaneous review and approval process with electronic communication of data among lenders, schools, and agencies. The delivery process most often concludes with electronic disbursement of funds to the student's school account. Students can typically view the status and progress of their application on the lender's or school's website, use an electronic signature for completing their promissory note, get an up-to-date reading on their borrowing, and receive online customized counseling regarding their rights and responsibilities as borrowers. Eventually, once in repayment, borrowers can also have electronic payments made to their loans directly from their employer's payroll system or through their own checking account. Efficiencies, standardized processes, and many other enhancements have created a relatively simple and seamless application and delivery process, and at least the appearance of a much less daunting overall set of steps and procedures. While this new efficiency is impressive and has resulted in a fairly painless process, borrowers should never lose sight of the fact that they are taking on a very major and serious obligation that will eventually require repayment and usually impact their lives for many years after they complete their degrees.

Background

Hundreds of lenders nationwide now offer educational loans, including those guaranteed by the federal government. Government-sponsored loans were originally called "Guaranteed Student Loans." Almost any student (U.S. citizen or permanent resident) enrolling in college could pretty much count on securing one (barring previous bad credit history). At the same time, the lender (usually a bank, credit union, or other financial organization), assuming it provided some level of due diligence in carrying out its responsibilities, would likewise be assured repayment by the government, even if the borrower defaulted. This program was created by the Higher Education Act of 1965 and has seen tremendous growth and remarkable success over its long history. Literally millions of students have received billions of dollars, and by far the vast majority of them have become more successful and more productive members of society and have also repaid their obligations in full. This is especially impressive when one considers that borrowers are typically very young and without any established credit, have no assurance of completing their education and securing employment, often change their original plans, and incur the obligation with no creditworthy co-signer required.

While many changes have taken place in this federal student loan program since its creation in 1965, the basic partnership between government and private resources has remained and continues to be the single largest student aid resource. One of the most significant revisions to the program, however, is worthy of note. Students have historically been required to demonstrate in some manner their *need* for the loan. The 1992 Reauthorization of the 1965 Higher Education Act made the loan program available to any student, regardless of family resources, by revising eligibility criteria. Except for a relatively brief period since the program's establishment, only students falling under certain income levels, or later only those "demonstrating financial need according to a federal formula," had been eligible to secure the funds. The major change in the 1992 legislation provided for an "unsubsidized" student loan to any otherwise eligible student. Unsubsidized borrowers enjoy most of the provisions of the student loan program, such as low interest rates (which would be capped regardless of the cost of money), deferred payment of principal, long-term repayment options, and government guarantees. However, the most significant distinction between those receiving "unsubsidized" versus "subsidized" loans is that unsubsidized borrowers do not have the support of interest subsidies paid on their behalf to the lender while they are enrolled as students and during other periods of deferment or grace. Instead, unsubsidized loans accrue interest during periods of enrollment that the borrower has to repay.

Interest Rates: Stafford Loans

In-School/Grace Period	Rate	Cap
Subsidized	0	0
Unsubsidized	1.7% + 91-day T-bill	8.25%

Repayment	Rate	Cap
Subsidized	2.3% + 91-day T-bill	8.25%
Unsubsidized	2.3% + 91-day T-bill	8.25%

The 91-day T-bill is reset annually on July 1. As of this writing, there is a proposal to set a fixed rate at 6.8% beginning in 2006. While this would be higher than rates in recent years, it would be lower than the historical average.

Repayment of this interest can be (and typically is) deferred until repayment begins, and this interest would then be added to principal, or "capitalized."

In-School Interest

Paying interest on unsubsidized loans while still in school avoids having this interest added to the loan principal (i.e., capitalized) when repayment begins. Depending upon the unsubsidized amount, if the amount of interest is relatively modest and the borrower can afford to repay it quarterly, the ultimate amount saved in additional interest could be significant.

Roughly one-third of borrowing in this government program has become unsubsidized.

Stafford FFELP Loans vs. Ford Direct Loans

The bank-based education loan program has become known as the Federal Family Education Loan Program (FFELP) and now provides both student loans (Stafford) as well as parent loans (PLUS Loans) for dependent students. The student loan program itself came under some serious attack in the early 1990s because of growing defaults, lack of standardization among lenders and state guarantor agencies (which had come to serve as intermediaries for the federal government), complexity and confusion, and excessive cost of administration. A major change in the program, again in the 1992 amendments, intended to address all of these problems by eliminating the "middlemen," primarily lenders and guarantors, and by applying the efficiencies that modern technology could provide. Institutions were offered a choice to remain with the bank-based program, also referred to as the Stafford FFELP Loan, or to move to a new "Ford Direct Loan" way of doing business. (Stafford and Ford are the last names of former members of the U.S. Congress who played leadership roles in authorizing federal student assistance.) Since that time, and as a result of this reform movement, significant enhancements and improvements have been made in the bank-based Stafford FFELP program, while the new Direct Loan program continues to provide schools with another option. Approximately 70 percent of institutions currently participate in the Stafford FFELP bank-based program, with the remaining 30 percent administering the Ford Direct Loan. In a few institutions where both programs are administered, some part of the institution (e.g., undergraduates) may be directed to one program, and others (e.g., professional students) to the other program.

The FAFSA

For either program, the borrower submits a federal application known as the Free Application for Federal Student Aid (FAFSA).

Selective Service Registration

Males between 18 and 25 years of age are not eligible for federal student aid, including student loans, unless they have registered for Selective Service. This may be done by checking a box on the FAFSA or online at www.sss.gov.

The application is available on the Web (www.fafsa.ed.gov), and applicants are encouraged to apply online, as the likelihood of making mistakes is reduced. You will need to indicate the name and federal identification code of the institution(s) to which the FAFSA data is to be sent. Codes may be found on the federal student aid website at www.studentaid.ed.gov or by calling 800-433-3243 (800-4-FED-AID). An acknowledgment called the Student Aid Report (SAR) is sent to the student filing the FAFSA, which provides an index called the "Expected Family Contribution" based on a formula (the federal methodology) used to determine federal aid eligibility. Institutions will advise you of your eligibility and whether they participate in the Direct Loan or in the Stafford FFELP bank-based program. If it is the bank-based program, you will typically be advised to select a lender from a list of one or more "preferred" lenders recommended by the school because of the school's positive evaluation of the products and services these lenders provide. Regardless of whether it is the Direct Loan or Stafford FFELP bank-based program, no further application is required, and you are asked to review and sign a promissory note. By law, the basic terms and conditions for both programs are virtually the same. Disbursements are made directly to your account at the school at the beginning of each term. Further details on current provisions are outlined below and can also be viewed on many institutional and participating lender websites, also referenced in the back of this book. Because provisions are subject to periodic change, check directly with lenders and schools for the most current terms. The calculation of an Expected Family Contribution is the result of a federal formula applied to the data submitted annually on the FAFSA. A detailed worksheet reflecting the step-by-step calculation is provided in Appendix A on page 161 and is also subject to annual revision. This Expected Family Contribution, or EFC, is then subtracted, along with any student financial aid, from the institution's cost of attendance. Other student financial assistance would generally include scholarships, fellowships, and grants from any and all resources, including other educational loans. Any remaining need would effectively become your eligibility, that year, for additional aid through student loan programs.

Because costs, family circumstances, and funding levels and eligibility criteria of programs are likely to change from year to year, a new application for financial aid, especially government and privately funded student loans, is required annually. The FAFSA can be submitted at any point after January 1 prior to the school year for which the funds are being requested. Students should keep a copy of their previous year's FAFSA to help them with the following year's application. The renewal FAFSA process has become as easy as ever, as the government offers an online "Renewal FAFSA," which requires the updating of only certain data elements.

It is very important to understand that institutions using the FAFSA may request additional information along with the FAFSA. If a school does, it should be so noted in its published procedures for determining financial aid eligibility and awards. While deadlines for government loan programs are relatively less restrictive, students should understand that institutional funds are limited and often distributed on a first-come, first-serve basis to those who meet the published deadline. When institutional funds are gone, they're gone. As a general rule of thumb, file no later than March unless the institution's deadline is earlier.

General Information for Federal Student Aid Eligibility

To receive aid from any of the federal student aid programs, you must meet *all* of the following criteria:

- Demonstrate financial need, except for some (e.g., unsubsidized) loan programs, as defined by the federal government

- Be enrolled or accepted for enrollment as a regular student working toward a degree or certificate in an eligible program

- Be a U.S. citizen or eligible noncitizen

- Have a valid Social Security number

- Meet satisfactory academic progress standards set by the school

- Certify that federal student aid will be used only for educational purposes

- Certify that you are not in default on a federal student loan and that no money is owed on a federal student grant

- Comply with the Selective Service registration (males only)

The law currently suspends aid eligibility for students convicted under federal or state law for sale or possession of illegal drugs.

The U.S. Department of Education verifies some of each applicant's information with the following federal agencies:

- Social Security Administration (for verification of Social Security numbers and U.S. citizenship status)

- Selective Service System (for verification of Selective Service registration status, if applicable)

- U.S. Immigration and Naturalization Service (for verification of eligible noncitizen status, if applicable)

- U.S. Department of Justice (for verification that an applicant has not been denied federal student aid by the courts as the result of a drug-related conviction)

- U.S. Department of Veterans Affairs (for verification of veteran status, if applicable)

STUDENT LOAN ELIGIBILITY

The major government loan opportunities are provided to eligible U.S. citizens or permanent residents through either the Direct Loan or the Stafford FFELP bank-based programs. Current loan limitations allow graduate and professional students to borrow up to $18,500 annually from these programs. Certain conditions and limits may impact each borrower's annual amount.

Another very important point needs to be made regarding "subsidy" benefits. Based upon your annual eligibility, which begins with the submission of the FAFSA, you may, during periods of academic enrollment on at least a half-time basis, have the interest on your loan amount up to $8,500 paid (i.e., subsidized) by the federal government. If you are not eligible for any part of this subsidy because of the results of the FAFSA or other factors, including the receipt of other forms of student financial assistance, you may still secure the $8,500 but without the subsidy. Again, this means that the interest on the loan will be accruing at the going rate and may be paid quarterly or, as is more often done, deferred until repayment begins, usually six months after you leave school.

Loan Deferments

Student loan payments are deferred for

- at least half-time study at an approved postsecondary school

- study in an approved graduate fellowship program

Student loan payments can also be deferred (or placed in "forbearance") in unusual conditions for up to three years for

- inability to secure full-time employment

- economic hardship

All of the interest on these loans, as well as that for future years' loans, will be added by most lenders (capitalized) all at once when the borrower enters repayment. The wise borrower should inquire specifically about the capitalization of interest prior to selecting a lender, to be sure such capitalization will occur only all at once and only upon the beginning of repayment.

All eligible borrowers may also request an additional $10,000 annually through this government program but will not be provided any interest subsidy, regardless of their eligibility for the subsidy on the first $8,500 of borrowing. This kind of loan is referred to as an "unsubsidized" loan. Both the initial $8,500 (subsidized or unsubsidized) and the $10,000 unsubsidized loan can be combined so that the student may borrow up to $18,500 annually to a maximum of $138,500 ($65,500 subsidized and $73,000 unsubsidized). This aggregate limit includes any money borrowed as an undergraduate. Students in health-related fields may borrow an extra $20,000. As will be noted with many aspects of this program, all of these current provisions are subject to change, and interested students are advised to secure more current information directly from lenders and institutions at the time of application.

Loan Limits: Stafford Loans Graduate/Professional Students	
Annual Limit	**Aggregate Limit**
Up to $18,500 each academic year (only $8,500 of this amount can be subsidized)	Up to $138,500 (only $65,500 of this amount can be subsidized; limit includes any amount received as an undergraduate)

- The government's FAFSA is the application form.

- Students apply annually for educational loans and must maintain satisfactory academic progress in order to remain eligible.

- Loan limits are subject to periodic change with new federal legislation.

LOAN FEES

Certain fees may be deducted by the lender from each loan you take upon disbursement. This is true for both the Direct Loan and the Stafford FFELP bank-based program. These "origination" and "guarantee" fees may amount to as much as 4 percent of the principal. At this time, there is some major shifting in lender/guarantor policy as to the charging of such fees. You should review carefully and ask about these fees as you check with your school and lender. As an extra incentive to choose certain lenders, some may offer to waive some or all of these fees or to refund them during repayment.

ONE LENDER

If a graduate or professional school student planning on borrowing has already taken on a government student loan as an undergraduate, it would most often be wise to continue borrowing from the same lender. This may not be possible in some cases for a variety of reasons, and in these situations, students would have an option upon completing their academic program to have all previous government loans from all lenders "consolidated." We discuss consolidation below. If borrowers holding outstanding previous government loans find themselves in a situation in which a new lender is needed, they should ask each potential lender whether it would be possible to consolidate the new loan with their previous loans when the time for repayment arrives.

OTHER FINANCING OPTIONS

Because most government loan programs have annual as well as aggregate borrowing limits, many students, especially those enrolled in professional programs, require additional financing beyond the current annual government limit of $18,500. These options are plentiful but should be pursued only if there are no other alternatives and the additional funds are absolutely needed. In considering private loan options, you should understand that loan consolidation options when repayment begins are currently restricted only to government loans. Many providers of private student loans do offer a "bundled billing" provision for those borrowers whose government loans and private loans were provided by the same lender. You should check carefully regarding this possibility by reviewing the information published by the lender, as well as by institutions participating in the Stafford FFELP program. Indeed, many institutions have developed and negotiated special arrangements with certain lenders, which include a "bundled bill" option. Of the many considerations that graduate borrowing entails, this is one of the most important and should be carefully researched *prior* to selecting a private lender.

Unlike most government loans, private loans do not have annual limits other than one that is restricted by the amount of the school's published annual cost of attendance, less any other student aid, including other student loans, which you may be receiving. In other words, you can't privately borrow more than the difference between what the school costs and how much aid—whether it be loans, fellowships, grants, or some combination of these—you're already receiving. Because there is no government subsidy or guarantee, private loans are also usually more expensive in terms of interest rates. They're also not typically protected by interest caps. You should carefully consider the longer-term risk posed by interest rates, which will typically change quarterly throughout the time the loan is outstanding, including through the repayment years, and which will be adjusted as the cost of money changes. This is one very significant difference between the government program and private loans.

A number of lenders also provide private educational loans customized to certain professions, such as law, business, and medicine. In addition to accommodating the special needs that these students may have during formal periods of enrollment, these loans may also offer assistance to those students preparing to take exams for accreditation or licensing, as well as for those involved in financing expenses related to residencies and even relocation.

PERSONAL FINANCING OPTIONS

In addition to government and private student loan programs, other forms of financing may be possible for certain students, especially those who are in a position in life where they may have accumulated some assets. Such possibilities for borrowing could include those that offer financing through equity in property, or from life insurance policies or even from certain retirement programs. Even though most students are not in such a position when they are considering graduate or professional school, for those who are so fortunate, the good news is that such borrowers would be repaying themselves with interest. Moreover, the interest in at least some of these scenarios could offer limited favorable tax considerations, effectively reducing the net cost of such financing. For those individuals who may find themselves with such alternate financing options, seeking professional advice from qualified tax consultants is recommended.

Even beyond the formal educational loans and the alternatives outlined above, some students may also have access to other forms of personal financing through special programs offered through their employers or their parents' employers; still others may have relatives willing to make special arrangements for personal loans. While such personal financing may be more limited and is not formally covered here, this kind of borrowing is being employed by some graduate and professional students.

OTHER GOVERNMENT LOANS

Even though the largest government loan volume is represented in the FFELP Stafford and Ford Direct Loan programs, there are other, more limited federal programs. One of these is the Perkins Loan (originally the National Defense Student Loan). While Perkins Loans are not as readily available as the FFELP Stafford and Ford Direct Loans because of limited funding, participating institutions do make this program available to eligible students. The application process for the Perkins Loan again begins with an annual filing of the FAFSA. Interest rates are currently fixed at 5 percent, and a standard 10-year repayment program begins following the student's graduation or withdrawal from graduate school. Perkins Loans may also be consolidated with other government student loans. The current annual Perkins Loan borrowing limit for graduate and professional school students is $6,000.

Perkins Loan Cancellation	
There are Perkins Loan cancellation provisions for certain forms of public service.	
Full-Time Career	**Amount Forgiven**
Teach in a designated elementary or secondary school serving students from low-income families	Up to 100%
Teach special education	Up to 100%
Provide qualified professional early intervention services for the disabled	Up to 100%
Teach math, science, foreign languages, bilingual education, or other subjects designated as teacher shortage areas	Up to 100%
Work in certain public service agencies serving high-risk children and families from low-income communities	Up to 100%
Become a nurse or medical technician, law enforcement and correction officer, or staff member in Head Start programs	Up to 100%
Volunteer with VISTA or Peace Corps	Up to 70%
Serve in the U.S. Armed Forces in areas of hostility or imminent danger	Up to 50%
More information on cancellation of Perkins Loans can be found at www.studentaid.ed.gov.	

Indeed, for individuals graduating from certain academic programs or from certain institutions, there may be special loan forgiveness opportunities. Students who borrowed through government programs and enter certain teaching careers may be able to have a percentage of their total obligation repaid for them for each year of full-time service.

FFELP Stafford and Ford Direct Loan Cancellation		
Cancellation Condition	**Amount Forgiven**	**Notes**
Full-time teacher for five consecutive years in a designated elementary or secondary school serving students from low-income families	Up to $5,000 of the aggregate loan amount outstanding after completion of the fifth year of teaching	Loan(s) must have been received on or after 10/1/98 by a borrower with no outstanding loan balance as of that date.
Further information regarding borrower eligibility and up-to-date listings of eligible schools considered as serving low-income students may be found at www.studentaid.ed.gov or by calling 800-433-3243.		

Other forms of government student loans are also available to eligible borrowers based upon their particular discipline, especially those students pursuing medical or health-related professions. Further information regarding eligibility, funding, application procedures, and other provisions is best secured from the institution.

Health Careers Loan Repayment Programs	
National Health Service Corps	**Nursing Education**
Certain forms of primary care in designated shortage areas	Service in eligible facilities in designated nurse shortage areas
Up to $25,000 each year for a minimum two-year commitment	Up to 60% of loan for two years of service Up to 85% of loan for three years of service
NHSC Loan Repayment Program Bureau of Primary Health Care 4530 East-West Highway, 10th Floor Bethesda, MD 20814 800-221-9393 www.bphc.hrsa.gov	Nurse Education Loan Repayment Program 5600 Fishers Lane, Room 9-36 Rockville, MD 20857 866-813-3753 www.bhpr.hrsa.gov/nursing/loanrepay.htm

Further information on such special programs should be sought directly from the institution's Office of Financial Aid.

REPAYMENT

Selecting a repayment plan for student loans, if such an option presents itself, should be done with some very careful considerations. Certainly among the more important of such considerations should be the ultimate cost of the loan. In most cases, the longer the length of repayment, the greater the ultimate cost of the loan. For example, if you were to take out $20,000 in Stafford loans and had to pay them off at the maximum variable interest rate of 8.25 percent in 10 years, you would make monthly payments of about $244, for a total cost of $29,236. If you were to pay off the same amount of loans at the same rate in five years instead, you'd have to make monthly payments of about $405, but the total cost would end up being $24,308. That's five grand you would save.

Sample Loan Repayment
Preliminary Projected Monthly Payment, Federal Stafford Program

Sample Interest Rate: 6.86%*

Amount Borrowed	Number of Payments	Estimated Monthly Payments	Recommended Annual Salary
$2,625	60	$50**	$7,500
$6,125	120	$71	$10,650
$11,625	120	$134	$20,100
$17,125	120	$198	$29,700
$23,000	120	$265	$39,750
$31,125	120	$359	$53,850
$39,625	120	$457	$68,500
$48,125	120	$555	$83,250
$56,625	120	$653	$97,950
$65,500	120	$756	$113,400

Recommended annual figures are based on 8% of gross income available for student loan repayment. Generally, manageable student loan payments range between 5% and 15% of income.

* Interest rate subject to change from year to year on Stafford loans

** Minimum payment of $50

In making arrangements for the repayment of government loans, lenders are required to offer borrowers various options. While more years to repay usually results in lower monthly payments, the additional years in delaying the final payment on the loan create additional financing cost to the borrower. In most cases, the early years of repayment typically find former full-time students faced with a number of expenses related to starting up their careers and their lives as truly self-supporting individuals. These could include down payments on cars, the need to invest in special equipment for their work, security deposits on apartments and utilities, the purchase of new business clothes, and similar expenses. These early costs can result in difficult choices. Too often the individual rushes into long-term solutions for spreading out loan repayments in order to meet monthly obligations, where in many cases a little control and frugality in lifestyle decisions in the first few years of being on one's own could more properly—and with far less expense—address the budget concerns without any serious impact. With patience and restraint, standard loan repayments can be absorbed and eventually become less of a burden as each year goes by, thus allowing the individual's lifestyle and quality of life to gradually improve. Nonetheless, current government provisions (always subject to change) do offer some significant measures of relief for borrowers whose total government student loan obligations are too excessive to shoulder in full at the start of repayment.

LOAN REPAYMENT OPTIONS

There are four available repayment plan options for government student loans. While there are slightly different provisions between the Stafford FFELP loans and Ford Direct Loans, the options generally are:

1. **Standard Repayment Plan**—fixed payments for up to 10 years.

2. **Extended Repayment Plan**—for borrowers whose education debt exceeds $30,000. Payment in either fixed or graduated payments may be extended for up to 30 years.

3. **Graduated Repayment Plan**—monthly payments are made on a plan in which these payments increase incrementally over the period of repayment, which could remain at 10 years or be extended for up to 30 years.

4. **Income-Sensitive Repayment Plan**—a repayment plan in which the payment is adjusted periodically based on the borrower's annual income, family size, interest rate, and loan amount. After 25 years, any remaining balance will be forgiven, but the amount forgiven is subject to taxation.

LOAN CONSOLIDATION

The consolidation of student loans has become a very attractive option in recent years. Current legislation allows the eligible borrower to secure a long-term fixed interest rate based upon a rate driven by the cost of money at the time—specifically (in repayment), the 91-day T-bill rate plus 2.3 percent. Eligible borrowers may currently lock in reduced rates on a permanent basis throughout repayment by arranging a federal government consolidation loan. The government changes the variable rate (it can go up or down) every summer (see below), and with rates currently at their lowest levels ever, consolidation is becoming a popular step to take. General information on student loan consolidation can be obtained from any participating FFELP lender or by contacting the U.S. Department of Education at 800-557-7392 or by visiting www.loanconsolidation.ed.gov.

Individuals (and their spouses) who have more than one type of government loan (e.g., FFELP, Perkins), have borrowed government loans from more than one lender, or believe they need relief from excessive monthly government student loan payments can combine (or consolidate) all of these obligations into one new loan and, equally important, one monthly payment. Consolidation loans may be arranged for repayment periods ranging from 10 to as many as 30 years. You would first want to consider keeping the standard 10-year schedule because you may enjoy even lower payments due to a possibly lower interest rate that may apply over the life of the loan.

Of course, comparing the new fixed interest rate to one that was originally agreed to and that might also be revised annually and subject to increase (or, again, decrease) each year through the repayment years is also important. Interest rates, regardless of how low they might be at any given time, will eventually rise. Government student loans currently secured in the Stafford FFELP program, even though capped, are subject to change annually on July 1, based upon various financial indices.

Loan consolidation can also provide for an easier payment process because the borrower is responsible for just one loan payment each month rather than a separate payment for each of several loans. All correspondence likewise is with only one lender. Married couples as well can arrange to have payments for each of their loans consolidated into one account. However, such consolidations could also present serious and permanent consequences to each individual in the event of the dissolution of a marriage.

Because each borrower's circumstances are different, it would not be wise to provide overly generalized suggestions for making consolidation decisions. Each borrower needs to decide if the lower monthly payment created by extending the loan beyond 10 years and the ease of dealing with only one lender is worth the additional finance charge. And you might be interested in investing your saved income rather than spending it on what is ultimately low-cost debt. In other words, if your money can earn you a greater rate of return in the stock market (or some other investment vehicle) than the rate you're paying on student loans, why not invest it? Would you rather your money work for you to increase your assets or decrease your debt? Making this decision will require some projection and calculation on your part. Generally, on the one hand, if you find that you'll make more money investing the money than you will spend on the increased finance charges of a longer repayment period, you should invest rather than pay down debt. On the other hand, old fashioned common sense would suggest that the elimination of debt as soon as possible is often a wise move.

Regardless of the number of years involved in a government loan consolidation, the interest costs should be limited to the new rate fixed at the time the refinancing decision is made. Under current laws there should be no origination fees, service charges, or prepayment penalties involved in arranging for a government consolidation loan.

Check with the lender for other forms of repayment arrangements, especially if the issue is one of temporary hardship due to underemployment or one-time expenses incurred early in your career. Such options for government loans include requesting periods of forbearance, arranging for lower payments for the first few years, and arranging for graduated payments that would increase over time. But again, all of these are possible while keeping the standard 10-year repayment plan.

> As of this writing, proposals in Congress under serious consideration would change government student loan consolidation provisions, including the one that allows variable loans to have a fixed, rather than a variable, interest rate. The current law allows government loans to be refinanced one time and fixed permanently at the prevailing rate at the time of consolidation, but that may no longer be true by the time you read this.

QUALITY AND STABILITY CONSIDERATIONS

Many of the long-term considerations that impact repayment can and should be addressed at the front end of the process, especially if you have a choice of lenders. Those institutions participating in the Stafford FFELP bank-based program often provide students with a list of preferred lenders from which to make a selection. Even though students ultimately have the right to select their own lender (unless the institution is involved with only one lender, such as in the federal Direct Loan), and even though the institution ideally is regularly and rigorously evaluating each lender's performance from A to Z, the wise borrower should ask some basic questions. For example, how long has the lender been in the business of providing student loans? What has been its historical commitment to the program? What is its current volume of borrowers and outstanding loans, and how long has it been at such a level? Because the "economies of scale" often produce cost efficiencies that can be passed on to the borrower in various ways, the size of the lender's volume might imply such potential efficiencies. There are, however, other important considerations.

Student lending has become a very large and profitable business for the banking industry, and many new players have entered the program in recent years. Some lenders may be seeking to attract and lure new borrowers with what appear to be lower rates and better provisions, at least at sign-up time. While such considerations are surely important, the impact of such a long-term financial obligation on your credit record will include your future opportunity to finance other important items, like a house; therefore, you should concern yourself with more than simply which lender might be offering a slightly cheaper product today. In addition to the legitimate concern for cost, you should also consider the *quality of service* the lender will provide, not only at the "front end," in terms of quick approvals and disbursements, but on the "back end" as well, especially during repayment years. Will the lender, for example, *hold* the loan through the school period, as well as through the last year of repayment? Or will the lender sell the loan to the highest bidder, who may later sell it again to yet another organization? Selling loans is not uncommon in the student loan world, but it does not necessarily imply that problems will occur. On the other hand, lenders who are committed to holding their student loans through repayment reflect a stronger commitment to the program and, more importantly, to the borrower. If the lender does indeed advise you that the loan will not be held, but sold, then you need to ask about who this new lender might be, whether future loans will be sold to the same new lender or others, when this transaction will occur, and whether it will cost *you*, the borrower, in any way.

Moreover, what is promised at the point of application in apparently very attractive terms is often based upon certain assumptions. One of the more common of these assumptions is that the borrower will not be even one day late in making monthly payments in the first 48 months after repayment begins. Based upon the borrower meeting this condition, the lender promises to reduce the interest rate by as much as 2 percent for the remainder of the repayment years. This indeed can result in significant savings for the borrower while serving as an incentive to keep the student loan from creating extra due diligence effort and cost for the lender. While this is clearly a very positive feature to consider, you should ask the lender for the number of borrowers who actually are benefiting from the provision. If the number is low, you should inquire as to why. If nothing else, the answer, not often reflected in the lender's promotional literature, could at least serve to educate you as to what needs to be done, as well as avoided, once repayment begins in order to gain the promised benefit.

Taking on the major and long-term obligation of a student loan is not something that should be done in a rush. If you begin the process far in advance of the start of school—usually three to four months is plenty of time, especially given today's technology—there should be ample opportunity to investigate the options and to ask basic questions. Government student loans, regardless of the lender, should generally be driven by basic provisions, which are fairly standard by law. What is not standardized is the lender's *long-term commitment*, quality of servicing, and overall stability in the student loan industry. If there appear to be less than clearly explained benefits; if there are omissions about important consumer issues not required by law, yet potentially very significant in the long run; or if there are promises made that sound almost too good to be true, then *buyer beware*. Other signs of caution may also be reflected by lenders who include in their marketing policies what many would consider overly aggressive solicitations for credit cards or other tactics that suggest the urgency of making a decision (e.g., a deadline after which certain special features may no longer be offered). By themselves, the various examples cited in this section may or may not be reasons to slow down and be concerned. But when the picture being painted has a rather common set of characteristics, then you may surely want to investigate other options, or at least start to ask some of the questions suggested above.

Because one of the educational institution's responsibilities is to regularly evaluate the quality of lenders, you should seek the good counsel and advice of your school's financial aid office. Some institutions have been able to arrange rather competitive provisions for their students, especially in respect to the private educational loan programs. Indeed, private educational lending often is provided by the same lender who offers the government loans. Special features may be made available in processing, provisions, and billing and loan servicing. All major quality lenders also provide dedicated customer service representatives and toll-free phone numbers, as well as online, real-time access to critical borrower information. You should investigate the quality of these important service considerations by actually trying them out prior to making any final selection of a lender. A full explanation of student loan borrower responsibilities and rights can be found in Appendix B.

BORROWING FOR EDUCATION

Borrowing money for any purpose should, of course, be done only with the utmost care and deliberation. An old rule of thumb is to borrow only when it is absolutely necessary and then to borrow only the amount needed. While the terms for interest, deferment, and repayment are very reasonable in comparison to other forms of financing, and even though the funds provided are also often limited only by what the institution defines as the cost of attendance (less any other student assistance), remembering the guidance of yesteryear about borrowing only when needed will always serve the wise borrower well once schooling is completed.

Education debt, unlike that taken on for the many consumer purchases made throughout one's lifetime, should be viewed as an *investment*, not as simply one more consumer debt. As with most long-term investments, there will most often be a lifelong *return* on this investment. Unlike many consumer purchases that begin to *depreciate* in value almost immediately upon purchasing them, the value of an education will most often continue to *appreciate* over one's lifetime. The statistics on this point are loud and clear.

Yes, we can all cite amazing stories of the high school dropout who went on to become a millionaire, as well as sad tales of the person who spent many years in school earning a PhD only to end up making a living driving a cab. But these are exceptions.

The economic well-being of a more educated individual in and of itself generally supports the broad contention that the value of education cannot be measured only in the cost required to secure it, but that it truly needs to be viewed with the long-term *return* perspective, which views this as an investment. There are, however, more and very significant kinds of returns for the individual investment that cannot as easily be measured in salaries and improved economic status. Well-documented research shows that the more educated a person is, most often also the longer the person's life span and the healthier the person's life will be. The same will likely be true of an educated individual's children, who will also more likely want and secure further education. More educated people also are more involved in their communities and are more civil to others. They are likewise less likely to be unemployed or convicted of crime.

Not only do individuals benefit in many ways, but so does society. Tax revenues needed to support basic government services are increased by a stronger level of productivity in its tax base; the cost of public assistance required for welfare, unemployment, and prisons is reduced; and communities, including the public service and public schooling they provide, are also enhanced by more active families and stronger financial resources.

BEING A WISE BORROWER

Strategies from Access Group®, a Nonprofit Student Loan Provider

Investing in Yourself

Your education is an important personal investment. Getting an advanced degree requires investing both time and money. You're spending your scarce resources now, in the hope that you'll achieve your personal, professional, and financial goals in the future. Achieving your goals, however, requires careful planning, especially if you'll be financing any portion of your educational investment with student loans.

Many students, particularly those pursuing professional degrees where graduate assistantships and fellowships typically are not available, need to take out education loans. Eligible students can borrow funds to cover the full cost of attendance established for their program of study by the school they're attending, less any other financial assistance they are receiving. The purpose of these loans, as with all financial aid programs, is to ensure that individuals are not prevented from achieving their goals because of their financial circumstances. It's all about access and opportunity.

Borrowing student loans to pay for your education can be an affordable financial decision. Student loans, particularly those guaranteed by the federal government, are lower in cost than most other forms of credit, and certainly are much lower than the cost of using credit cards. They also have an array of flexible repayment options to accommodate your particular financial circumstances (including the ability to temporarily postpone making payments if necessary).

If you're like most students, you'll be repaying your education loans with your future income. This will reduce the amount of disposable income you'll have available to pay for your expenses once you're out of school. You'll also be using that income to pay your other debts, such as from credit cards, your living expenses, and to invest for your retirement. Being able to pay for all the things you want once you graduate and being able to successfully achieve your future goals requires that you make wise borrowing decisions both while in school and after you have completed your degree.

Wise Borrower Strategies

By taking a proactive approach and exercising prudent borrowing strategies, you can help ensure success in meeting your personal and professional objectives affordably. The following five strategies can help you become a wiser borrower:

- Identify and document your goals

- Make well-informed choices

- Borrow the minimum amount you need to achieve your goals

- Maintain accurate financial records

- Establish and maintain a strong credit history

IDENTIFYING YOUR GOALS

It's important to identify and document your long-term personal, professional, and financial goals. Answering the following questions can help you establish and achieve these goals.

- How do I want to use what I plan to learn?

- What do I want to accomplish in my career?

- Where do I want to work?

- Where do I want to live?

- What kind of lifestyle do I want?

- What hopes do I have regarding a family?

- When do I want to retire?

- What kind of lifestyle do I want once I retire?

- How much will I need to earn to achieve my goals?

Recording your answers to these questions is important so that you can gauge your progress in achieving them. You also should review your goals from time to time so that you can update them as your circumstances change. For example, if you get married, you may want to re-examine your goals to be certain they are consistent with those of your spouse.

MAKING WELL-INFORMED CHOICES

The cost of your education is up to you. How much you "spend" getting your degree depends on the choices or decisions you make. For example, the cost of tuition depends on the school you choose, the cost of housing depends on where you choose to live and whether you live alone or with one or more other people who can share the cost with you, the cost of food depends on your eating habits and where you choose to eat. Once you make a choice, you must pay the required cost. As such, you're responsible for the choices you make. No one else can claim that responsibility—not your parents, not your friends, not your siblings, not your financial aid administrator, not your faculty advisor. Think carefully about what you'll have to give up once you're working in order to pay back the debt you incurred because of the choices you made as a student. Be certain you'll be willing to make the required sacrifices before you spend borrowed funds while in school.

BORROWING THE MINIMUM

The key to borrowing the minimum amount you need to achieve your objectives is to make certain you're adhering to an affordable in-school budget. Your budget should give you a clear understanding of your current financial status, including your available resources, your planned educational expenses, and the financial commitments you've made before entering school that will remain once you matriculate.

Once you have developed your in-school budget, you should be able to determine how much you'll need to borrow. Will you be able to afford to repay this amount once you graduate? Answering this question can be an effective motivator in helping you minimize your in-school borrowing. Finding the answer requires that you also estimate your future out-of-school budget, comparing your future income to your anticipated expenses. As long as your future income is sufficient to pay for your future lifestyle, including repayment of your student loans and setting aside adequate reserves for the future, then you probably can afford what you plan to borrow. If not, you should carefully consider making some adjustments to your in-school budget so that you can reduce what you'll have to borrow (and what you'll ultimately need to repay).

Although your future income is an important factor in determining what constitutes manageable payments on your student loans, it's not easy to predict with certainty how much you'll be paid once you complete your degree. There are resources, however, that can help. Your school may have career-planning staff who can provide realistic starting salary information for your discipline or chosen profession as well as important employment planning information.

Another useful resource is the Internet. There are several general employment sites you may want to explore for more information on starting salaries, including www.salary.com, www.monster.com, and www.job-web.com. The career profiles on www.princetonreview.com also are a great resource! In addition, check the websites of any professional organizations that are affiliated with your planned career or profession.

Once you have an idea of a realistic starting salary, estimate how much of that salary will be available to spend on your lifestyle. Certain items will be deducted automatically from your paycheck (taxes, employee benefits, etc.). Then you have to take care of your debts, such as your student loan payments, car payment, and credit card bills. The remainder is what you'll have to meet your living expenses, including housing, food, transportation, insurance, clothing, entertainment, and your long-term savings and investment needs.

When it comes to savings and investments, do you know how much you should be setting aside? Financial planners often recommend that you have at least six (6) months worth of your monthly expenses in savings in case you lose your job and/or have some other financial emergency. Similarly, they recommend that individuals invest at least 10 percent of their gross monthly earnings starting at age 21 if they hope to retire at age 65 with the same lifestyle in retirement that they had when they were working.

So, will your income be enough to cover all these expenses, including your estimated monthly student loan payments? Will your projected out-of-school budget be in balance, or will you have a surplus or deficit? A budget surplus can be handled without difficulty; you always can spend more (perhaps by saving or investing it for the future). But a projected deficit will be a problem; it means you're spending more than you have available to meet all your expenses. Eliminating this anticipated deficit will require that you either increase your available resources or spend less (or perhaps both).

One way to reduce, if not eliminate, the projected deficit is to borrow less while in school so that you'll have less to repay once you graduate. For example, you should strive to live as cheaply as possible while you're a student. It's been said that if you live like a professional while you're in school, you may have to live like a student once you graduate. So, try living below your means while in school. Be thrifty! The less you spend now, the more you'll have later, during the early years of your career. Following are some ideas on how to be thrifty as a student:

- Live with roommate(s)

- Take your lunch; bring your own coffee (and/or other beverages)

- Eat at cheap places when dining out

- Dress for less

- Clip and use coupons

- Have "free fun": take advantage of on-campus entertainment, go to matinees, rent and share videos

- Don't buy a new car; use public transportation; car pool; ride a bicycle

- Avoid impulse buying; always shop with a list

- Beware of buying for "convenience," such as having food delivered

- Refrain from taking on further consumer debt, such as from credit cards; don't charge more on your credit cards than you know you will repay each month when the bill arrives

Another means of reducing your need to borrow is to consider ways in which you can increase your non-loan financial resources to pay your expenses. You could work part-time. Be certain, however, that this employment does not interfere with your educational progress and success. Working can reduce what you have to borrow as well as provide you with an opportunity to gain valuable experience in your chosen field.

You also should consider applying for scholarships and grants offered by private organizations, foundations, and associations to supplement any funding you already are receiving from the school you plan to attend. Staff at the school may be able to guide you on where to apply for these programs.

Whatever you do, remember that you should be financing your education in a manner that will allow you to succeed in achieving your goals without producing a financial future that results in personal budget deficits once you get out of school. As you make your borrowing decisions, it's important to distinguish between what you have to pay for and what you want to pay for.

MAINTAINING ACCURATE FINANCIAL RECORDS

You should keep copies of all documents relating to your financial activities. At a minimum you should retain the following items:

- Loan documents (applications, promissory notes, disbursement and disclosure statements, loan transfer notices, lender correspondence)

- Receipts for major purchases (computer hardware and software, appliances, furniture, cars, any items with warranties)

- Income tax returns and all the documentation used to prepare those returns (federal, state, and local, as applicable)

- Estate planning documents, including your will

It's important to save all of your student loan documents and correspondence so you know exactly what you've agreed to, what's expected from you as a borrower, and how much you've borrowed. It may not seem important at the beginning of the student loan process, but when you're closer to repayment, you may need to refer to some or all of these documents. Keep all student loan-related documents and correspondence until all education loans have been fully repaid.

You should also keep a log or journal of all conversations with the lender(s) and servicer(s) of any loans you borrow. This log should include the date and time you called, the reason for the call, any expected follow-up, and the full name of the person with whom you spoke. You can maintain a notebook-style log or maintain the log on your computer. Whatever form you use, your log may come in handy if there is a dispute about the conversation at some later date.

When setting up your recordkeeping system, be sure it's easy to use, a system you'll maintain over the life of the loan, and secure from theft or fire. There are many books and software products on personal finance to help you get started. Whether you use file folders, portfolios, binders, or envelopes, it's a good idea to set up one folder for each type of loan or account and keep the items sorted accordingly.

ESTABLISHING AND MAINTAINING A STRONG CREDIT HISTORY

Never underestimate the value of good credit. If you'll need to borrow a private student loan to attend graduate or professional school, as many students do, your credit history likely will impact your ability to obtain the funds you need. When you apply for a private student loan, the lending institution or creditor will probably request a copy of your credit report and credit score from an authorized credit reporting agency. This information will be used to help determine if you qualify for the loan, and if so, influence what you'll pay for the funds. You must demonstrate a good credit history to be approved for most private student loans as well as other forms of credit such as home mortgages, auto loans, and business loans.

Most graduate and professional degree students applying for private education loans today have already established a credit history. You have a credit history if you have at least one credit card, consumer loans such as auto loans, student loans, or any other form of personal credit. Credit histories are derived from repayment records reported by creditors and other organizations (such as financial institutions, major retail stores, lenders, landlords, and utilities) to authorized credit reporting agencies, such as the three national credit bureaus: Equifax, Experian, and Trans Union. These records are examined by lenders to determine if credit should be extended to you. The fundamental issue for the lender is your "willingness to repay the loan," that is, the likelihood that you'll repay the loan based on your past credit performance.

Your credit report is a summary of your credit history. Just as your academic transcript is a history of the courses you've taken and how you've performed in those courses, your credit report can be viewed as your credit transcript because it lists the credit you have obtained (by individual account) and how you've managed that credit.

Another measure often used to quantify how well you've managed your credit obligations is credit scoring. Credit scoring is a quick, accurate, consistent, and objective method of determining the likelihood that you'll repay a future loan. Fair, Isaac and Company (FICO) first developed the credit scoring methodology and currently is the largest provider of credit scores to lenders. The "credit score" is a numerical forecast that focuses on individual borrower behavior. It is based on information in your credit report. You want to have the highest possible score.

Factors that influence your credit score include promptness in paying bills; total debt; amount owed on all credit card accounts; age of credit accounts; number of credit card accounts; total available credit card limit; the proportion of credit card balances to total available credit card limit; number of credit card accounts opened in the past 12 months; number of finance accounts; and occurrence of negative factors such as serious delinquency, derogatory public records, collection accounts, bankruptcies, student loan defaults, and foreclosures. The following credit tips can help you maintain the highest possible credit score:

- Pay all your bills on time.

- Minimize your credit card debt; keep credit card balances to no more than 30 percent of your available credit limit.

- Avoid charging more than you can afford to repay.

- Check your credit report (and credit score) at least once a year from each of the three national credit reporting agencies; promptly correct any errors that you find on your reports.

- Limit the number of credit card accounts you maintain.

- Be careful about opening new credit card accounts and closing older ones; it is beneficial to have the longest possible history regarding the age of your credit card accounts.

- Notify your creditors immediately whenever your address changes.

BECOMING A WISE BORROWER

Your education is an important key to your financial future and to your success. It is an investment in which you can take great pride. Becoming a wise borrower need not be painful or time consuming. Making practical, common-sense decisions using the best possible information should allow you to achieve your educational goals without sacrificing your financial future. But you must manage your resources carefully by making well-informed choices, forming good financial habits, developing a budget that you can afford, borrowing the minimum needed to complete your degree, and managing the repayment of that debt responsibly.

Access Group is a nonprofit organization that has specialized in graduate and professional student lending for over 20 years. It offers a complete family of federal and private loans that includes post-graduate loans and federal loan consolidation. Access Group also provides debt management materials, online budget and loan repayment calculators, as well as other related services.

800-282-1550   accessgroup.org

PART 4

Decisions, Bad Decisions, and Bottom Lines

Money Management

We have some very simple, common-sense suggestions to help frame your approach and direct your lifestyle while you're in grad school. Certain steps will reduce the distraction that financial difficulties and pressures often create and allow you to focus more properly on the important educational matters at hand. Controlling spending to the basic necessities will also serve to lower the need for financing and thus provide the basis for a less restricted lifestyle once you've assumed your full-time job, whatever it ends up being. As challenging as frugality may be during school, such constraints are not nearly as frustrating as not being able to provide for a reasonable lifestyle for yourself and your family because of burdensome student loan or credit card payments incurred by unnecessary choices made in graduate school. This long-term perspective, often blurred by the myriad temptations confronting most students of all ages, should be the primary view by which all financial decisions are made.

NEEDS VS. WANTS

Restraint begins on the cost side of whatever formula is used to determine what might be needed for further schooling. The fewer the expenses, the less the requirement for financing, including the use of credit cards. While there is little or no flexibility with the direct expenses of tuition and fees, most graduate and professional students have some reasonable level of options for housing and food. Similar discretion is most often available for other personal needs, including transportation. The guiding principle with deciding on these non-tuition and fee expenses should be to know the difference between a *need* and a *want*. Some expenses will be fixed, such as rent, but surely can range considerably. Your place should be convenient to the school and to the resources, both human and material, needed to pursue your degree—in other words, the places where you conduct the research or fulfill the responsibilities that you've been assigned. Finding a suitable roommate with whom to share rent and utilities is also a simple way of reducing your expenses. Besides, sharing is a virtue. Another basic expense, food, also offers a wide range of flexibility. Meal plans provided by universities typically provide, for a modest cost, balanced nutrition and the convenience of not having to shop, prepare, and clean up afterward. You usually have a variety of meal plans from which to choose, and while eating three solid meals a day for seven days a week may be the ideal, not all of these meals necessarily need to be procured through a formal meal plan. Some meals can easily be prepared in one's residence, especially breakfast and lunch. While these suggestions may appear to be rather prosaic, the other extreme of eating all meals in restaurants would surely present a much more expensive approach. Eating out is one of those choices—or *wants*—that can add considerably and unnecessarily to the cost side of the equation.

Of course, there will be other expenses for clothing, laundry, and insurance. For students whose insurance is no longer covered by family plans, institutions most often will be able to provide group policy rates for health insurance. Trying to get through graduate or professional school without such insurance is very risky and could, if needed and not in place, result in financial problems so serious that continued schooling may have to wait.

One of the most expensive items that you can control is transportation. Reasonable transportation allowances are provided in the cost-of-attendance expense budget of the institution. Not included in this allowance are car payments. Adding excessive or even unnecessary car payments, including the cost of insurance and maintenance, to your budget while in school is another one of those wants that quickly add to the financial pressures that detract from your focus as a student.

CREDIT CARDS

Not on the list of basic expenses for graduate and professional school is the payment of credit card debt. As suggested earlier in this publication, individuals who face the challenge of paying for graduate or professional school already have a significant burden to shoulder, assuming they start with a "clean slate"—that is, no significant debt. Trying to meet monthly payments for credit card debt incurred prior to beginning graduate school, or incurring credit card debt for unnecessary wants after returning to school, is a recipe for trouble. Credit cards should be used in graduate school only as a last resort. And if they are used, they should be paid off every month. You should operate on a cash basis as much as possible. Managing your credit and paying bills on time will be a very important factor in securing future credit for the many major purchases in life. Prior to beginning graduate or professional school, you should completely pay off all credit card debt.

The misuse of credit cards too often results in financial disaster. Charging the maximum line of credit can lead quickly to the inability to make payments—the classic credit trap. Interest rates can reach as high as 23 percent if payments are not made in full each month. A rule of thumb, then: If the item is not needed, avoid buying it. Some warning signs of credit card overuse include: reaching the maximum credit line allowed, increasing rather than decreasing monthly balances, using funds from one credit card to make payments on another, paying for basic needs of food and monthly utilities by credit card, or using more than 15 percent of one's monthly income to pay credit card debt. Prior to beginning graduate or professional school, if any of these signs applies to you, reconsider grad school until they are addressed. In such serious circumstances, you should seriously consider seeking advice from a financial consulting organization about restructuring or refinancing your debt in order to reduce monthly obligations and to preserve your good credit status. You can call 800-388-2227 for the location of such an agency near you. The nonprofit National Foundation for Consumer Credit can offer assistance in directing such individuals to agencies organized to help review the circumstances and provide advice that might help in refinancing.

Prior to beginning each academic year, wise graduate students should create a simple budget worksheet that lays out the direct and indirect expenses for the period of enrollment on one side of a page. On the other side of the page, they should list the resources from all sources that will be available. Resources could include family support; student aid in the form of fellowships, scholarships, grants, loans, and part-time work during the school year; and savings from vacation periods or from other personal resources. If the expenses far exceed the resources and all reasonable efforts to resolve them prove fruitless, your attendance may have to be deferred or reduced, or certain wants reduced, or advice sought from the institution's financial aid office prior to finalizing enrollment plans. If you need a reasonable amount of additional student aid, you're more likely to get it if your request is initiated far in advance of the start of the school year. Even though financial aid officers may be able to address unexpected emergencies, the lack of reasonable preparation on a student's part does not typically equate to an emergency. Moreover, seeking student aid resources to solve past or current unnecessary choices may not be possible.

FINAL THOUGHTS

We can't overstate this: Financing solutions are relatively painless to secure for most graduate students *but should be undertaken with great care*. Borrowing only what is needed will mean lower monthly payments in the future. Simply because you're eligible for the maximum allowed in the student loan program does not mean that you need to borrow the maximum. While some lenders suggest that manageable student loan payments may range between 5 and 15 percent of income, the line you should follow is that monthly student loan obligations should not exceed 8 percent of gross monthly income once you're out there in the working world. (See Sample Loan Repayment, page 130). And if you're making enough money as soon as you get out of school to make standard repayments (within this 8-percent-of-income parameter), you should do so. If such payments exceed 12 percent of monthly income, then some of the alternate payment options available, including, but not limited to, formal loan consolidation, should be considered.

Demonstrating previous good money management will not only serve you well later in life, but could also enhance opportunities for successful admission, enrollment, and graduation. The ability to demonstrate a clean credit history is a reflection of your sense of personal responsibility. Some professional schools require a copy of an applicant's credit report during the admission process. They'll partly base their financial aid offer on your credit history. If you have a negative record, it could jeopardize the school's ability to secure the needed financing for you to complete the program and thus potentially result in a denial of enrollment. If you have any question about your individual credit record, investigate it prior to applying to school. If a problem exists, you may have time to correct it. There are three major credit reporting agencies, each of which will have a record: Equifax (800-685-1111, www.equifax.com), Experian (800-682-7654, www.experian.com), and TransUnion (800-888-4213 or 800-916-8800, www.transunion.com). In order to learn more about understanding a credit report, check the general information available on the websites of each of these organizations. In some cases, one agency's records may be in error or differ significantly from another's. Addressing such issues prior to seeking financing for grad school would, of course, be prudent.

You may find yourself in a situation where quitting your job may be impossible for a variety of reasons. Or it may be convenient for you to pursue an advanced degree on a less-than-full-time basis. Indeed, your employer may even offer tuition reimbursement benefits upon your successful completion of a course. While part-time enrollment surely involves more time and less focus on academic pursuits, it's been successfully done by many professionals. Because more institutional resources are often dedicated to those pursuing full-time enrollment, some scholarship and fellowship opportunities won't be as available to part-time students, if at all. There are still some limited possibilities, however, and inquiry about such resources should be made directly with each school's admissions office. Government loans are available to at least half-time students (as defined by each school's registrar) enrolled in a degree-granting program. Many lenders also offer private student loans to those enrolled at less-than-half-time status. Again, the institution would be the best source of information about such financing options.

Possible Tax Benefits

The Internal Revenue Service (IRS) is responsible for administering the tax code as authorized by federal legislation. Because tax laws are subject to change quickly, the information provided in this section is more general in nature. The best advice and most current guidance on various tax considerations is most often found by checking with experienced and recognized tax advisors.

The Taxpayer Relief Act of 1997 (TRA '97) created some very favorable benefits for eligible U.S. federal tax filers who can claim certain kinds of education expenses incurred by themselves or by dependent members of their families. Beginning in 1998, eligible taxpayers could claim a Lifetime Learning Credit for qualifying expenses incurred for any postsecondary education, including graduate and professional school. There is no limit on the number of years this credit may be claimed, but it may not be claimed in the same year that the student receives a tax-free withdrawal from an Education IRA.

You can claim a below-the-line federal income tax credit for 20 percent of qualified tuition and fees for yourself, your spouse, and your dependents. The credit cannot be claimed for expenses incurred for books, room and board, or other incidentals. Before calculating the credit, however, the taxpayer must deduct any fellowship, scholarship, and other tax-free financial assistance, including a distribution from an Education IRA and employer-provided education assistance. Financial assistance received from recognized student loans is not considered. Beginning in 2003, the maximum yearly credit you will be able to claim is $2,000 (20 percent of $10,000), again not to exceed 20 percent of qualified tuition and fees. The Lifetime Learning Credit is taken for the year the expenses are paid and for education that begins either that year or in the first three months of the following year. Even students pursuing a graduate or professional program on a less-than-half-time basis are eligible to take the credit. It is not available to all tax filers, only to those who fall under certain income caps. For married couples filing a joint return, the current Adjusted Gross Income (AGI) cutoff is $100,000. For those filing a single return, the current income cap is $50,000. The amount of the credit is gradually reduced and eventually phased out, based upon actual income.

The same legislation (TRA '97) also authorized the deduction of qualified education loan interest, again for eligible U.S. federal income tax filers. (For your personal eligibility, the best counsel is obtained from professional tax experts.) Beginning in 2001 the maximum amount of student loan interest a borrower could deduct was increased to $2,500 a year. There are currently also AGI ceilings for the deduction: To qualify for the full deduction, married couples filing jointly must make less than $100,000 and single filers must make less than $50,000. The deduction is also gradually phased out for those with an AGI between $65,000 and $130,000 (joint) or between $50,000 and $65,000 (single). The deduction is not available to individuals with an AGI of $130,000 or higher (joint) or $65,000 or higher (single).

Qualified loans include federal education loans (Stafford FFELP and Direct, PLUS, Perkins, Federal and Direct Consolidation Loans, and healthcare profession loans), as well as education loans issued by schools, banks, and not-for-profit associations. Personal loans undertaken for education, including those from family members, do not qualify for the tax deduction.

Unlike the limitation for the Lifetime Learning Credit, which restricts consideration to tuition and fees, the education loan for which interest has been paid could have been incurred to pay for related education expenses, including tuition, fees, books, and room and board, at least to the extent reflected in the institution's published cost of attendance. In accordance with IRS regulations, the education-related expenses must have been paid within a reasonable period of time before or after the debt was incurred, as well as attributed to education during a period when the recipient was an eligible student. As with the Lifetime Learning Credit, the taxpayer must first subtract the amount of any scholarships or other educational assistance from the qualifying educational expenses *before* calculating the tax deduction. To help the qualifying taxpayer review possible tax benefits, the lending institution should send the borrower an annual statement (Form 1098-E) indicating the amount of interest paid that is eligible for the tax deduction consideration.

The TRA '97 does provide some very favorable tax considerations for eligible federal income tax filers. It should be noted that there is a basic and significant difference between the tax *credit* for the Lifetime Learning program and the tax *deduction* of education loan interest. The former could literally reduce the tax liability of the filer, while the latter reduces the filer's income upon which the tax obligation is determined. Again, because these laws are subject to change with new legislation at any time, and because of the intricacies of the tax code and the fact that each student's situation is different, the best advice should be sought from qualified tax professionals. The current tax code providing these favorable considerations is written to expire in 2010, but lobbying efforts to make them permanent beyond this date are already under way. For the most current information visit the IRS website, www.irs.gov, and download Publication 970, *Tax Benefits for Education*.

Finally, each educational institution should be able to provide a student account statement from which the amount of qualified tuition and fees can be calculated. Again, while credit cannot be claimed for tuition expenses paid with tax-free funds (scholarships, fellowships, grants), *it can be claimed for tuition paid for with loans*. In the case where both sources (scholarships, etc., and loans) of funds are used to pay for both tuition and housing expenses, all tax-free aid is presumed by the IRS to be *applied to tuition expenses first*. The exception to this rule would be a scholarship or grant specifically designated by the grantor to be used for housing, books, or other nontuition expenses.

Grad School Financial Aid Crib Sheet

- ◆ Research programs and career paths

  - Know your own credentials and be realistic

  - Focus on long-term goals

  - Decide full time or part time

  - Include any possible personal constraints

  - Identify and prepare for entrance exam

  - What is best program and route for you?

- ◆ Apply

  - Submit application as required by institution

  - Have all previous college transcripts sent

  - Submit portfolios if appropriate

  - Request solid letters of recommendation

  - Include application fee

  - Visit prospective school(s)

  - Have realistic admission sights

  - Develop a "Plan B" if not accepted

- ◆ Cost

  - Understand basic differences: public, private, out of state, in state

  - View cost as long-term investment with return

  - Investigate possible employer-reimbursed program

  - Be realistic about finances, lifestyle, money management

  - Note distinction between graduate vs. professional school viewpoints

♦ Options for Paying

- Institutional scholarship, assistantships, fellowships, stipends

- Consider duration and sources of support, including government

- If necessary, investigate educational loan opportunities

  Government

  Private

  Other financing options, if available

  If borrowing, consider long-term issues

  Quality of lending organization

  Consolidation

♦ Money Management

- Focus should be academic and basic needs

- Control lifestyle and choices

- Come with clean slate

- Careful use of credit cards

♦ Other Thoughts

- Tax considerations and possible benefits

- Constant changing nature of basics

  Costs

  Programs

  Funding levels and eligibility criteria

We began by talking about the rather clear-cut advantages of additional schooling, and it's fitting that we should end with them: the farther you go with your education, the more likely you are to be better off in life. The most evident indication of this typical improved life is the generally increased lifetime earnings of the individual (see page 48). Many other benefits come with graduate degrees, including improved health and longevity, a better appreciation of life and the ability to enjoy it, the probable college aspirations of your children, and a more likely involvement in your community and profession, often in a leadership role. While securing a graduate or professional degree is not a fail-safe guarantee of such benefits, it most often will be a fairly safe bet.

We hope we have provided encouraging suggestions about what is involved, how good planning can help ensure success, and how to avoid potential pitfalls. Now go out there and apply them and get on with the beginning of the rest of your life!

PART 5

Worksheets and Resources

Expected Family Contribution

Worksheet A: The Annual Net Cost of Graduate School

School Offer

1. Academic Year Stipend $ _____

2. Summer Stipend $ _____

3. Tuition Scholarship (AY and summer) $ _____

4. Student and Out-Of-State Fees $ _____

5. Health Insurance $ _____

6. Professional Development $ _____

7. **Total In** $ _____

School Expenses

8. Living Expenses $14,000

9. Geographic Adjustment for Cost of Living $ _____

10. Educational Expenses $1,400

11. Student Fees $ _____

12. Tuition $ _____

13. Health Insurance $ _____

14. FICA, Medicare, Union Dues $ _____

15. Federal, State, and Local Withholding Tax $ _____

16. **Total Out** $ _____

17. ANNUAL NET GAIN OR LOSS $ _____

Explanations

1. It is important to know how many years this stipend is guaranteed (assuming satisfactory academic progress) and how much work is involved. Both impact your time to degree.

2. Scientists and engineers are often supported in the summer by their faculty advisor's research grants. Social scientists and students in the

humanities and arts often have to fend for themselves. Twelve months of effort towards the degree results in a shorter time to degree.

3. How many years is this guaranteed?

4. Many schools tack hefty fees onto the tuition bill. Find out how many are covered by the tuition scholarship.

5. Health insurance can be very expensive (>$1000/yr) especially if you are trying to cover a family. Find out how much it is and how much the university will supplement the expense.

6. Doing research and then publishing it can be expensive. What departmental funds or university grants are available to do your work if your faculty advisor does not have research funding for you?

7. This is what the university will provide towards the annual cost of earning the degree.

8. We estimate that room ($5,500), food ($2,400), transportation ($2,400), and personal expenses ($3,700) will be about $1,200 a month for a Notre Dame graduate student. Add $7,000 for a spouse and $3,500 per child.

9. It costs far more to live in Boston than it does in South Bend. Check a cost of living index to adjust your living expenses accordingly. You can find a couple on the web (www.infoplease.com/ipa/AO883960.html, www.lib.umich.edu/govdocs/steccpi.html#cities) or ask a graduate student going to the school of your choice how much rent, food, etc cost.

10. We estimate that it costs about $1000 a year in text and reference books, supplies, and computer-related expenses. When your coursework is done, the money you spent on books will be used to go to professional meetings.

11. These may run up to several hundred dollars and be assessed up-front at the beginning of every term.

12. Don't forget out-of-state costs if that applies.

13. You have to think not only about the insurance premium but the personal cost of deductibles and uncovered items (e.g., dental, optical, allergie medications). The federal government is banking on the idea that you will spend less than 5% of your income on medical expenses (or you can begin deducting from your income taxes).

14. This money isn't coming back no matter how much you cheat on your taxes.

15. Most of this money should come back in a lump sum after you submit your income tax forms.   It is important, however, to know how much actual take-home pay you get every month to live on. A current grad student, claiming the same number of exemptions will be the best source of information.

16. This is how much it will cost per year to get the degree.

17. This is how much you will have left over (an unlikely scenario) or how much you will need to get to stay in school full-time. Spousal income, student loans, parental gifts, and part-time jobs are the usual sources.

Expected Family Contribution:
Independent Students with Dependents
(2004–2005 Academic Year)

Contribution from Income (Student's and Spouse's)

1. Student's (and Spouse's) Adjusted Gross Income $ _____

2. Student's (and Spouse's) Untaxed Social Security Benefits $ _____

3. Student's (and Spouse's) Veteran's Noneducational Benefits $ _____

4. Student's (and Spouse's) Other Untaxed Income and Benefits. This may include child support received, workers' compensation, earned income credit, disability payments, welfare benefits, tax-exempt interest income, cash support from others, and housing, food, and living allowances for military, clergy, or others $ _____

5. Deductible IRA, KEOGH, 403(b), and 401(k) payments made by student (and spouse) $ _____

6. **Total Income**. Add Lines 1 through 5 $ _____

7. U.S. Income Taxes paid $ _____

8. State Income Taxes paid $ _____

9. Social Security Taxes paid $ _____

10. Child Support paid by you for another child $ _____

11. Hope Tax Credit, Lifetime Learning Credit, Americorps awards, taxable earnings from Federal Work-Study (or other need-based work program) and other student financial aid that may have been included in Line 6 $ _____

12. Income Protection Allowance from Table A $ _____

13. Employment Expense Allowance. If both student and spouse work, enter 35% of the lower income or $3,000, whichever is less. If student qualifies as a single head of household, enter 35% of that income or $3,000, whichever is less $ _____

14. **Total Allowances**. Add Lines 7 through 13 $ _____

15. **Student's (and Spouse's) Available Income**. Line 6 minus Line 14 $ _____

Contribution from Assets (Student's and Spouse's)

16. Cash, savings, and checking accounts $ _____

17. Net worth of real estate (excluding primary residence), investments, stocks, bonds, trusts, commodities, precious metals, college savings plans $ _____

18. Business and/or Commercial Farm Net Worth from Table B $ _____

19. **Total Assets**. Add Lines 16 through 18 $ _____

20. Asset Protection Allowance. From Table E $ _____

21. Discretionary Net Worth. Line 19 minus Line 20 $ _____

22. **CONTRIBUTION FROM ASSETS.** Multiply Line 21 by 12% $ _____

23. Adjusted Available Income. Add Line 15 and Line 22 $ _____

24. **TOTAL CONTRIBUTION**. From Table D. If negative, enter 0 $ _____

25. Number in College Adjustment. Divide Line 24 by the number in college at least half-time at the same time. Quotient is the contribution/students $ _____

Expected Family Contribution:
Independent Students without Dependents
(2004–2005 Academic Year)

Contribution from Income (Student's and Spouse's)

1. Student's (and Spouse's) Adjusted Gross Income $ _____

2. Student's (and Spouse's) Untaxed Social
   Security Benefits $ _____

3. Student's (and Spouse's) Earned Income Credit $ _____

4. Student's (and Spouse's) Other Untaxed Income and
   Benefits. This may include workers' compensation,
   disability payments, cash support from others,
   tax-exempt interest income, welfare benefits,
   housing, and food and living allowances for military,
   clergy or others $ _____

5. Deductible IRA, KEOGH, 403(b), and 401(k)
   payments made by student (and spouse) $ _____

6. **Total Income**. Add Lines 1 through 5 $ _____

7. U.S. Income Taxes paid $ _____

8. State Income Taxes paid $ _____

9. Social Security Taxes paid $ _____

10. Income Protection Allowance of $5,490 for single
    students or married students if both are enrolled in
    college at least half-time; $8,780 for married
    students if only one is enrolled at least half-time $ _____

11. Child Support paid by you for another child $ _____

12. Hope Tax Credit, Lifetime Learning Credit,
    Americorps awards, taxable earnings from
    Federal Work-Study (or other need-based work
    program) and other student financial aid that may
    have been included in Line 6 $ _____

13. Employment Expense Allowance. If the student is single, enter $0. If the student is married and both the student and spouse are working, enter 35% of the lower income or $3,000, whichever is less. Otherwise, enter $0 $ _____

14. **Total Allowances**. Add Lines 7 through 13 $ _____

15. **Available Income**. Line 6 minus Line 14 $ _____

16. **Contribution from Income**. Take 50% of Line 15 $ _____

Contribution from Assets (Student's and Spouse's)

17. Cash, savings, and checking accounts $ _____

18. Net worth of real estate (excluding primary residence), investments, stocks, bonds, trust, commodities, precious metals $ _____

19. Business and/or Commercial Farm Net Worth from Table B $ _____

20. **Total Assets**. Add Lines 17 through 19 $ _____

21. Asset Protection Allowance. From Table E $ _____

22. Discretionary Net Worth. Line 20 minus Line 21 $ _____

23. **CONTRIBUTION FROM ASSETS.**
    Multiply Line 22 by 35%. If negative, enter $0 $ _____

24. **TOTAL CONTRIBUTION**. Add Line 16 and Line 23 $ _____

25. Number in College Adjustment. Divide Line 24 by the number in college at least half-time at the same time. Quotient is the contribution/students $ _____

Table A—Income Protection Allowance	
Family Members (Including Student)	**Allowance**
2	$13,700
3	$17,060
4	$21,070
5	$24,860
6	$29,070
Each Additional	$3,280

Note: *For each student over one in college, subtract $2,330 from the appropriate maintenance allowance.*

Table B—Adjustment of Business/Farm Net Worth	
Net Worth of Business/Farm	**Adjustment**
To $100,000	40% of Net Worth
$100,001 to $295,000	$40,000, plus 50% of NW over $95,000
$295,001 to $490,000	$137,500, plus 60% of NW over $295,000
$490,001 or more	$254,500, plus 100% of NW over $490,000

Note: *Table C data is omitted because it relates primarily to undergraduate, dependent student information.*

Table C—Independent Student Contribution	
Available Income (AA)	**Contribution**
Less than $3,409	– $750
– $3,409 to $12,200	22% of AA
$12,201 to $15,400	$2,684 plus 25% of AA over $12,200
$15,401 to $18,500	$3,484 plus 29% of AA over $15,400
$18,501 to $21,600	$4,383 plus 34% of AA over $18,500
$21,601 to $24,700	$5,437 plus 40% of AA over $21,600
$24,701 or more	$6,677 plus 47% of AA over $24,700

Table E—Asset Protection Allowance (Independent Student)					
Age	**Single**	**Married**	**Age**	**Single**	**Married**
25 and under	$0	$0	46	$20,100	$43,200
26	$1,200	$2,500	47	$20,500	$44,200
27	$2,300	$5,000	48	$21,000	$45,300
28	$3,500	$7,400	49	$21,500	$46,500
29	$4,700	$9,900	50	$22,000	$47,900
30	$5,900	$12,400	51	$22,600	$49,100
31	$7,000	$14,900	52	$23,100	$50,300
32	$8,200	$17,400	53	$23,700	$51,800
33	$9,400	$19,800	54	$24,200	$53,100
34	$10,600	$22,300	55	$24,800	$54,700
35	$11,700	$24,800	56	$25,400	$56,000
36	$12,900	$27,300	57	$26,100	$57,700
37	$14,100	$29,800	58	$26,700	$59,400
38	$15,300	$32,200	59	$27,500	$61,200
39	$16,400	$34,700	60	$28,100	$63,000
40	$17,600	$37,200	61	$28,900	$65,200
41	$18,100	$38,100	62	$29,800	$67,100
42	$18,400	$39,100	63	$30,600	$69,000
43	$18,900	$40,100	64	$31,400	$71,300
44	$19,200	$41,100	65 or older	$32,300	$73,700
45	$19,700	$42,100			

Borrower Responsibilities and Rights

Responsibilities

When you take out a student loan, you have certain responsibilities. Here are some important ones.

- When you sign a promissory note, you're agreeing to repay the loan according to the terms of the note. The note states that except in cases of loan discharge, you must repay the loan, even if you don't complete your education (unless you couldn't for a valid reason— because the school closed, for example). Also, you still must repay your loan if you can't get a job after you complete the program, or if you don't like or don't receive the education you paid for.

- Think about what your repayment obligation means before you take out a loan. If you don't repay your loan on time or according to the terms in your promissory note, you might go into default, which has very serious consequences and will affect your credit rating.

- You must make payments on your loan even if you don't receive a bill or repayment notice. Billing statements (or coupon books) are sent to you as a convenience, but you're obligated to make payments even if you don't receive any reminders. You must also make monthly payments in the full amount your repayment plan has established. Partial payments do *not* fulfill your obligation.

- If you apply for a deferment or forbearance, you must continue to make payments until you're notified the request has been granted. If you don't, you might end up in default. You should keep a copy of any request form you submit, and you should document all contacts with the organization that holds your loan. You must notify the loan servicer when you graduate, withdraw from school, or drop below half-time status; change your name, address, or Social Security number; or transfer to another school.

  — If you take out a Perkins Loan, either the school that lends you the money or an agency the school employs will service your loan.

  — If you take out a Direct Loan, the Direct Loan Servicing Center will service your loan.

  — If you borrow under the FFEL Program, your lender or its servicing agent will service your loan. During your loan counseling session, you'll be given the name of the loan servicer(s).

- Regardless of the type of loan you borrow, you must receive entrance counseling before you're given your first loan disbursement, and you must receive exit counseling before you leave school. Your school will provide the counseling and important information about your loan. Your lender will give you additional information.

Rights

You have certain rights as a borrower. Listed below are some of them.

- Before your school makes your first loan disbursement, you'll receive the following information about your loan from your school, lender, and/or the Direct Loan Servicing Center:

  — The full amount of the loan

  — The interest rate

  — The date you must start repaying the loan (based on the anticipated graduation date recorded on the promissory note)

  — A complete list of any charges you must pay (loan fees) and information on how those charges are collected

  — Information about the yearly and total amounts you can borrow

  — Information about the maximum repayment periods and the minimum repayment amount

  — An explanation of default and its consequences

  — An explanation of available options for consolidating or refinancing your loan

  — A statement that you can prepay your loan at any time without penalty

- Your school must notify you in writing whenever it credits your account with Stafford Loan or Perkins Loan funds. This notification must be sent no earlier than 30 days before and no later than 30 days after the school credits your account. You may cancel all or a portion of the loan by informing your school within 14 days after the date your school sends this notice, or by the first day of the payment period, whichever is later. (Your school can tell you the first day of your payment period.) If you or your parents receive loan funds directly by check, the funds may be refused by returning the check.

- Before you leave school, you'll receive the following information about your loan from your school, lender, and/or the Direct Loan Servicing Center:

  — The amount of your total debt (principal and estimated interest), what your interest rate is, and the total interest charges on your loan

  — If you have FFELs, the name of the lender or agency that holds your loans, where to send your payments, and where to write or call if you have questions

  — If you have Direct Loans, the address and telephone number of the Direct Loan Servicing Center

  — An explanation of the fees you might be charged during the repayment period, such as late charges and collection of litigation costs if you're delinquent or in default

  — An explanation of available options for consolidating or refinancing your loan

  — A statement that you can prepay your loan without penalty at any time

If you borrow a Federal Perkins Loan, your school will provide this information to you. If you borrow a Direct Loan or FFEL, the Direct Loan Servicing Center or your lender will provide this information to you, respectively.

  If you have Direct or FFEL Stafford Loans, your school will also provide the following information during exit counseling:

  — A current description of your loans, including average monthly anticipated payments

  — A description of applicable deferment, forbearance, and discharge provisions

  — Repayment options

  — Advice about debt management that will help you in making your payments

  — Notification that you must provide your expected permanent address, the name and address of your expected employer, and any corrections to your school's records concerning your name, Social Security number, references, and driver's license number (if you have one)

- You have the right to a grace period before your repayment period begins. Your grace period begins when you leave school or drop below half-time status.

- Your school, lender, and/or the Direct Loan Servicing Center, as appropriate, must give you a loan repayment schedule that states when your first payment is due, the number and frequency of payments, and the amount of each payment.

- You must be given a summary of deferment and discharge (cancellation) provisions, including the conditions under which the U.S. Department of Defense might repay your loan.

- If you or your parents borrow under the FFEL Program, you must be notified when the loan is sold if the sale results in making payments to a new lender or agency. Both the old and new lender or agency must provide this notification and provide the identity of the new lender or agency holding the loan, the address to which the borrower must make payments, and the telephone numbers of both the old and new lender or agency.

The Student Guide,
Financial Aid from the U.S. Department of Education,
2003–2004

Glossary

Assistantship: financial assistance to help in meeting living and uncovered educational expenses provided to a student in return for, in most cases, career-related work.

Borrower: a person to whom a loan has been made. For education at the graduate and professional level, lenders provide government-guaranteed loans as well as nongovernment loans; in some cases, the federal government itself is the lender.

Capitalization: an increase in the principal balance of a student loan that takes place when the lender adds the interest accrued on the loan to the outstanding balance, effectively changing this interest to principal.

Collection: action taken by an authorized organization or agency to recover a loan for which a borrower has defaulted.

Consolidated Repayment Plan: an option provided by the federal government that allows borrowers to combine certain eligible federal loans into a single new loan with one lower monthly payment over a 10-year or extended repayment period. If the monthly payment is extended, the total amount of interest repaid by the borrower could be greater than under the standard 10-year repayment plan, depending upon the new interest rate for the consolidated loan.

Consolidation: when certain federal student loans are combined into one new loan from one lender. The repayment period may be extended beyond the original plan, depending on the amount borrowed, but does not have to be. The new loan may have an adjusted interest rate less than or greater than the original, depending on current government legislation.

Cost of Attendance: an estimate of the typical student's education-related expenses for a given period of enrollment at a particular institution. These expenses include direct costs as billed by the institution and indirect costs incurred by students enrolled in the program, including modest allowances for personal and transportation needs.

Credit Check: a review of a borrower's (and co-signer's, where applicable) credit information.

Default: when the borrower fails to meet his or her obligation to repay for 270 days and the guarantor concurs that the borrower does not plan on satisfying the repayment obligation. Legal action may be taken to collect on a defaulted loan.

Deferment: a period of time during which a borrower is permitted to postpone student loan repayment under certain conditions and without cost or penalty. In the case of unsubsidized loans, interest will continue to accrue during deferment at the borrower's expense.

Delinquent: a student loan the day after a borrower fails to meet a full loan payment on the agreed-upon due date.

Direct Loan: an education loan with reasonable interest rates and long-term repayment provisions made available by the federal government through eligible participating institutions for eligible students enrolled on at least a half-time basis.

Disbursement: the transfer of the proceeds of a student loan by check, master check, or electronic funds transfer (EFT) from a lender to the school at which the student is enrolled or plans to enroll.

Entrance Interview: a formal presentation to the borrower of his or her rights and responsibilities related to the government student loan being awarded. This must be done for the borrower by the institution in which he or she is enrolled or via the Web as established by the institution in accordance with government regulations and often with the assistance of the authorized lender.

Exit Interview: a formal presentation to the borrower of his or her rights and responsibilities related to the government student loan that had been awarded. This includes information on the total amount borrowed, the name of the lender and guarantor, the repayment schedule and interest rate, and options for deferment, cancellation, and consolidation.

Expected Family Contribution (EFC): the estimate of a student's family's ability to contribute toward the Cost of Attendance. This is used to determine a student's eligibility for need-based federal student assistance.

Extended Repayment: a student loan repayment plan that allows the borrower to repay over a period ranging from 12 to 30 years, depending on the amount of the loan. Whenever a loan repayment plan extends beyond the standard schedule, the borrower will pay more interest.

Federal Methodology: a formula set by Congress that calculates the Expected Family Contribution (EFC) used to determine eligibility for need-based federal student assistance. Data for this process are furnished by the student annually on the Free Application for Federal Student Aid (FAFSA).

Fellowship: The definition of a fellowship will vary with the sponsor. Most often, it means a stipend and a full tuition scholarship without a service (teaching) requirement.

Financial Aid Office: the office within an institution that helps to direct students to resources needed to help make the cost of attendance affordable. In the case of graduate and professional student aid, this office may be centralized for the entire institution or be decentralized and focused solely on the needs of a particular academic program.

Financial Need: the difference between the individual student's cost of attendance and Expected Family Contribution. This concept is employed by institutions in administering any need-based student assistance, including that provided by the federal government.

Forbearance: a limited period of time during which a borrower is allowed to cease making principal payments or to reduce these payments. During periods of forbearance, the borrower is responsible for the interest that accrues.

Free Application for Federal Student Aid (FAFSA): the application required for determining eligibility for federal (and in some cases state) financial assistance. Applicants ask that their FAFSA data be sent to the school they plan to attend, which in turn advises the applicants of their eligibility. The FAFSA is available on the U.S. Department of Education's website (www.ed.gov/prog_info/FSA/FAFSA) and may be submitted electronically.

Grace Period: the period of time that begins as soon as the student stops being at least a half-time student and ends on the date on which the first payment on a student loan is due. For most government loans, this period is six months.

Graduated Repayment Plan: a repayment plan for a student loan in which the amount of the payment is scheduled to change (usually increase) during the repayment period. The period of repayment cannot exceed 10 years, excluding any grace, deferment, or forbearance periods.

Guarantor: a state or private not-for-profit organization that agrees to reimburse the lender under certain conditions for borrowers who have defaulted on their repayment obligations.

Guarantee Fee: a fee charged by the agency guaranteeing each loan it guarantees. Sometimes also referred to as an "insurance fee," the rate cannot exceed 1 percent under current law and is sometimes reduced by the lender who remits the fee to the guarantor.

Holder: any organization that owns the promissory note signed by the borrower of a student loan. Lenders sometimes sell loans to other organizations (other lenders or secondary markets), effectively transferring the promissory note. In such cases, the borrower must be advised by federal law, and the terms remain unchanged.

Income Sensitive Repayment Plan: a student loan repayment schedule agreed to by certain borrowers whose expected total monthly gross income falls below certain levels during the course of repayment. Monthly payments are adjusted annually based upon the borrower's actual income.

Independent Student: All graduate and professional students applying for federal student aid are considered to be independent of their parents. Some schools reserve the right to request parental information and cooperation in administering their own institutional student aid resources, even for graduate and professional students.

Insurance Fee: the fee charged to borrowers by the organization or agency insuring the student loan; also known as a "guarantee fee."

Lender: the organization, including the federal government, providing the funds for a student loan.

Master Promissory Note (MPN): a formal and legally binding agreement between the borrower and the provider of a student loan in which the borrower agrees to pay the loan, with interest, in periodic installments. The language in the note includes important information regarding periods of grace, deferment, and forbearance as well as possible cancellation provisions. Equally important information on the borrower's rights and responsibilities for the loan is also provided. The borrower should read the MPN carefully before signing it.

Origination Fee: the fee charged to borrowers by lenders. This fee is used to help reduce the costs of the program. For federal student loans, this fee is set by and paid to the federal government by the lender. The fee was authorized by Congress, is subject to adjustment periodically, and is currently 3 percent.

Repayment Period: the period of time in which loan payments are required and during which interest accrues on the borrower's outstanding balance.

Repayment Schedule: a plan for repaying the loan and the interest in which the number of installments and the amount of each payment is detailed through the final payment until the loan is paid in full. Information is also provided on the interest rate, the due date for the first and all subsequent payments, and the frequency of installments.

Research Assistantship (RA): an assistantship that provides the student with a stipend for doing research with and for a faculty member. The amount of the stipend will vary by discipline, sponsor, and/or institution.

Satisfactory Academic Progress: the level of academic standing and progress required by a student in order to remain eligible for government student loans. Each institution is responsible for monitoring this achievement by standards it defines for qualitative and quantitative academic good standing.

Scholarship: sometimes referred to as "tuition scholarship" or "tuition waiver"; grant assistance ranging from partial to full cost of tuition that does not require payback or, in most cases, any form of service or employment. It is typically not subject to taxation, either.

Secondary Market: an organization that buys loans from lenders, thus allowing the lender to make more loans. Not all student loan lenders sell their loans.

Servicer: an organization responsible for performing certain functions related to determining the status of a student loan. These functions include deferment and forbearance processing, billing services during repayment, and collection activities for delinquent loans. Some lenders perform their own servicing and others employ other organizations to do this, in which case all borrower-lender correspondence is with the loan servicer.

Stafford Loan: an education loan with reasonable interest and long-term repayment provisions made available from the federal government through private lenders on behalf of eligible students enrolled at least half-time in eligible institutions.

Standard Repayment Plan: a repayment schedule for a student loan in which the borrower agrees to pay equal amounts for each monthly payment throughout the entire repayment period or to pay an amount that is adjusted annually to reflect changes in a loan's variable interest rate. A standard repayment plan cannot be longer than 10 years or 120 monthly payments but can be less, depending on the amount borrowed. This limit excludes periods of grace, deferment, or forbearance.

Stipend: regular financial support throughout the school year, usually on a monthly basis, to help pay for living expenses beyond tuition and fees.

Student Aid Report (SAR): a report sent to students who submit a Free Application for Federal Student Aid (FAFSA). The SAR provides the applicant with an opportunity to review the accuracy of the data originally submitted and provides the student with an eligibility index or Expected Family Contribution (EFC). The institution, which also receives this information, uses the student's EFC along with other information to determine his or her federal student aid eligibility.

Subsidized Student Loan: a long-term, low-interest education loan in which the interest on the loan is paid not by the borrower during periods of grace or deferment but rather by another party, usually the government but in some cases another organization such as the institution.

Teaching Assistantship (TA): an assistantship that provides the student with a stipend for teaching responsibilities ranging from providing support services such as laboratory work, grading papers and exams, guest lectures, and tutoring to designing and teaching courses.

Unsubsidized Student Loan: a long-term, low-interest education loan provided to students who do not qualify for financial aid but still need additional financing for their college expenses as determined by the institution in which the student enrolls or plans to enroll. In some cases, eligible students may receive both a subsidized and an unsubsidized loan, as long as annual and aggregate loan limits are not exceeded. Unlike subsidized loans, however, the borrower is responsible for the interest that accrues during periods of grace and deferment. In these cases, the borrower can choose to have this interest deferred until repayment begins, at which time the interest is capitalized and added to the principal.

Resources for Prospective Graduate Students

Sources of Information Concerning Graduate Student Life and Demographics

Choy, S.P., S. Geis, and A.G. Malizio. *Student Financing of Graduate and First-Professional Education, 1999–2000*. U.S. Department of Education Document NCES 2002-166, 2002.

Hoffer, T.B., B.L. Dugoni, A.R. Sanderson, V. Welch, I. Guzman-Barron, and S. Brown. *Doctorate Recipients from United States Universities: Summary Report 2001*. National Opinion Research Center, University of Chicago, 2002. (Visit www.norc.uchicago.edu/studies/sed/sed2001.htm.)

Lovitts, Barbara. *Leaving the Ivory Tower: The Causes and Consequences of Departure from Doctoral Study*. Rowman and Littlefield Publishers, Inc., 2001.

Sources of Information for Graduate Programs

American Universities and Colleges. 16th ed. Walter de Gruyter, Inc., 1998.

Doughty, Harold R. *Guide to American Graduate Schools*. 8th ed. Viking Penguin Books, 1997.

ERIC Clearinghouse on Higher Education is an online resource for graduate school research information. Visit www.eriche.org.

GradSchools.com is an online resource for graduate school information at www.GradSchools.com.

Sources of Information for Professional Programs

ADEA Official Guide to Dental Schools. 39th ed. American Dental Association Publishers, 2002. Visit www.adea.org.

Gilbert, Nedda. *Complete Book of Business Schools*. The Princeton Review/Random House, 2003.

Health Professions Career and Education Directory. American Medical Association Press, 2003–2004. Visit www.ama-assn.org.

Owens, Eric. *Complete Book of Law Schools*. The Princeton Review/Random House, 2003.

Stoll, Malaika. *Complete Book of Medical Schools*. The Princeton Review/Random House, 2003.

Graduate Program Rankings

Maher, Brendan, ed. *Research-Doctorate Programs in the United States*. National Academy Press, 1995.

U.S. News & World Report: *Best Graduate Schools*. 2004 ed.

Sources of Information for Mastering Standardized Entrance Exams

GRE

Guest, Deborah. *Cracking the GRE Biology Test.* The Princeton Review/ Random House, 2002.

Jay, Meg. *Cracking the GRE Psychology Test.* The Princeton Review/ Random House, 2002.

LaBerge, Monique. *Cracking the GRE Chemistry Test.* The Princeton Review/Random House, 2002.

Leduc, Steve A. *Cracking the GRE Math Test.* The Princeton Review/ Random House, 2002.

Lurie, Karen. *Crash Course for the GRE.* The Princeton Review/Random House, 1999.

Lurie, Karen, Adam Robinson, and Magda Pecsenye. *Cracking the GRE with Sample Tests on CD-ROM.* The Princeton Review/Random House, 2003.

McMullen, Doug, Jr. *Cracking the GRE Literature Test.* The Princeton Review/Random House, 2002.

Wu, Yung Yee. *Verbal Workout for the GRE Exam.* The Princeton Review/ Random House, 1997.

TOEFL

Buffa, Liz, and Laurice Pearson. *Cracking the TOEFL with Audio CD, International Edition.* The Princeton Review/Random House, 1998.

Miller, George S. *Cracking the TOEFL with Audio CD.* The Princeton Review/Random House, 2002.

GMAT

French, Doug. *Verbal Workout for the GMAT*. The Princeton Review/ Random House, 1999.

Martz, Geoff, and Adam Robinson. *Cracking the GMAT with CD-ROM*. The Princeton Review/Random House, 2002.

Schieffer, Jack. *Math Workout for the GMAT*. The Princeton Review/ Random House, 1998.

Still, Cathryn. *Crash Course for the GMAT*. The Princeton Review/Random House, 2000.

MCAT

Flowers, James L., and Theodore Silver. *Flowers and Silver MCAT*. The Princeton Review/Random House, 1997.

———. *Flowers and Silver Practice MCATs*. The Princeton Review/Random House, 1998.

LSAT

Robinson, Adam, and Rob Tallia. *Cracking the LSAT with Sample Tests*. The Princeton Review/Random House, 2002.

Funding Sources

Blum, Laurie. *Free Money for Graduate School*. 4th ed. Facts on File, Inc., 2000.

Cassidy, David. *The Scholarship Book*. Prentice Hall Press, 2002.

Hamel, A.V. *The Graduate School Funding Handbook*. University of Pennsylvania Press, 2002.

Richards W.A., ed. *Scholarships, Fellowships, and Loans*. 17th ed. Gale Group, 2001.

Websites

www.studentaid.ed.gov	Federal student aid information
www.ed.gov/prog_info/SFA/FAFSA	Help in completing FAFSA
www.bls.gov/oco	U.S. Department of Labor Occupational Outlook
www.americorps.org	Information about Americorps Program awards
www.todaysmilitary.com	Financial aid opportunities through U.S. Armed Forces
www.gibill.va.gov	Educational benefits through U.S. Department of Veterans Affairs
www.ftc.gov/scholarshipscams	Information regarding fraudulent scholarship searches
www.ifap.ed.gov	Worksheets to calculate Expected Family Contribution (EFC)
www.bhpr.hrsa.gov/nursing/loanrepay.htm	Health profession loan forgiveness information
www.dl.ed.gov	Direct Loan information
www.ed.gov/Programs/bastmp/SGA.htm	U.S. Department of Education for guaranty agency information
www.loanconsolidation.ed.gov	Direct Loan Consolidation information
www.salliemae.com	FFELP loan information
www.usafunds.org	Managing student debt information
www.norc.uchicago.edu/issues/docdata.htm	National survey of earned doctorates
http://distance.gradschools.com	Consortium of physical and virtual universities
www.usnews.com	Ranking of graduate programs by subdiscipline
www.gre.org/pracmats.html	GRE test preparation material
http://grediagnostic.ets.org	Fee-based enhanced service for GRE test preparation

www.kaptest.com	Tips on developing test-taking skills
www.gre.org/cbttest.html	Arranging GRE test
www.toefl.org	Information regarding Test of English as a Second Language (TOEFL)
www.mba.com	Information regarding attending business/management school
www.LSAC.org	Information regarding Law School Admissions Test (LSAT)
www.peacecorps.gov/gradschool	Information regarding fellowship assistance for Peace Corps volunteers
www.usuhs.mil	Information regarding medical school assistance for members of U.S. Armed Forces
www.collegeboard.com	Source of general financial aid information
http://ace.nd.edu/ace	Information about a two-year service program at the University of Notre Dame
www-rotc.monroe.army.mil	General information about Army ROTC Scholarships
www.afrotc.com	General information about Air Force ROTC Scholarships
www.navy.mil	General information about Navy ROTC Scholarships
http://defenselink.mil	Links to all U.S. Armed Forces websites

Dozens of websites are also provided in part 3 of this publication, which lists some, but not all, of the fellowships available on a competitive basis from sources outside the university.

About the Authors

Peter Diffley received his BS in biology at Tulane University, an MA at the University of Montana, and his PhD at the University of Massachusetts. After six years of graduate school, he was awarded an NIH post-doctoral fellowship to do research at the Yale Medical School. He then spent three years as an assistant professor at Texas Tech and six years at the University of Notre Dame. As a faculty member in the Department of Biological Sciences, he served on the graduate admissions committee, on many dissertation committees, and in several faculty search committees. In 1990, Dr. Diffley became an associate dean in the Graduate School at Notre Dame. He oversees university tuition scholarships, fellowships, and assistantships and helps students in their search and application for outside fellowship support. He is past chair and current treasurer of the Association of Graduate Schools in Catholic Colleges and Universities and past chair of the Midwest Association of Graduate Schools.

Joseph A. Russo came to Notre Dame as Director of Financial Aid in 1978 after serving in similar capacities at Le Moyne College and Genesee Community College in upstate New York. His responsibilities were expanded in the autumn of 2002 when he was appointed as the Director of the Office of Student Financial Services. He is a graduate of Le Moyne and Syracuse University.

Russo, who is in his 39th year as a financial aid administrator, has served as a consultant to a number of organizations, including the College Board and the U.S. Department of Education, and as the editor of the National Association of Student Financial Aid Administrators'(NASFAA) *Journal of Student Financial Aid*. He has written extensively on various student aid issues and received his profession's distinguished Golden Quill Award in 1998 for literary and research contributions to the student aid world he has served for so many years. He was a charter member of the NCAA Committee on Financial Aid and Amateurism and has testified before the U.S. Senate and the House on major public policy issues related to student aid. He also has been involved in training and teaching throughout his entire career, including serving for more than 20 years as the primary instructor in a graduate-level course at Notre Dame on student aid administration.

Notes

Notes

Graduate School Entrance Tests

Business School

Is an MBA in your future? If so, you'll need to take the GMAT. The GMAT is a computer-based test offered year round, on most days of the week. October and November are the most popular months for testing appointments. Most business schools require you to have a few years of work experience before you apply, but that doesn't mean you should put off taking the GMAT. Scores are valid for up to five years, so you should take the test while you're still in college and in the test-taking frame of mind.

Law School

If you want to be able to call yourself an "esquire", you'll need to take the LSAT. Most students take the LSAT in the fall of their senior year—either the October or the December administration. The test is also offered in February and in June. The June test is the only afternoon administration – so if your brain doesn't start functioning until the P.M., this might be the one for you. Just make sure to take it in June of your junior year if you want to meet the application deadlines.

Medical School

The MCAT is offered twice each year, in April and in August. It's a beastly eight-hour exam, but it's a necessary evil if you want to become a doctor. Since you'll need to be familiar with the physics, chemistry, and biology tested on the exam, you'll probably want to wait until April of your junior year to take the test— that's when most students take the MCAT. If you wait until August to give it a shot, you'll still be able to meet application deadlines, but you won't have time to take it again if you're not satisfied with your results.

Other Graduate and Ph.D. Programs

For any other graduate or Ph.D. program, be it art history or biochemical engineering, you'll need to take the GRE General Test. This is another computer-based test, and, like the GMAT, it's offered year-round on most days of the week. The most popular test dates are in late summer and in the fall. Take the test no later than October or November before you plan to enter graduate school to ensure that you meet all application deadlines (and the all-important financial aid deadlines) and to leave yourself some room to take it again if you're not satisfied with your scores.

Understanding the Tests

MCAT

Structure and Format

The Medical College Admission Test (MCAT) is a six-hour paper-and-pencil exam that can take up to eight or nine hours to administer.

The MCAT consists of four scored sections that always appear in the same order:

1. Physical Sciences: 100 minutes; 77 physics and general chemistry questions

2. Verbal Reasoning: 85 minutes; 60 questions based on nine passages

3. Writing Sample: two 30-minute essays

4. Biological Sciences: 100 minutes; 77 biology and organic chemistry questions

Scoring

The Physical Sciences, Biological Sciences, and Verbal Reasoning sections are each scored on a scale of 1 to 15, with 8 as the average score. These scores will be added together to form your Total Score. The Writing Sample is scored from J (lowest) to T (highest), with O as the average score.

Test Dates

The MCAT is offered twice each year—in April and August.

Registration

The MCAT is administered and scored by the MCAT Program Office under the direction of the AAMC. To request a registration packet, you can write to the MCAT Program Office,
P.O. Box 4056, Iowa City, Iowa 52243
or call 319-337-1357.

GRE

Structure and Format

The Graduate Record Examinations (GRE) General Test is a multiple-choice test for applicants to graduate school that is taken on computer. It is a computer-adaptive test (CAT), consisting of three sections.

- One 30-minute, 30-question "Verbal Ability" (vocabulary and reading) section

- One 45-minute, 28-question "Quantitative Ability" (math) section

- An Analytical Writing Assessment, consisting of two essay tasks

    o One 45-minute "Analysis of an Issue" task

    o One 30-minute "Analysis of an Argument" task

The GRE is a computer-adaptive test, which means that it uses your performance on previous questions to determine which question you will be asked next. The software calculates your score based on the number of questions you answer correctly, the difficulty of the questions you answer, and the number of questions you complete. Questions that appear early in the test impact your score to a greater degree than do those that come toward the end of the exam.

Scoring

You will receive a Verbal score and a Math score, each ranging from 200 to 800, as well as an Analytic Writing Assessment (AWA) score ranging from 0 to 6.

Test Dates

The GRE is offered year-round in testing centers, by appointment.

Registration

To register for the GRE, call 1-800-GRE-CALL or register online at www.GRE.org.

Understanding the Tests

LSAT

Structure and Format

The Law School Admission Test (LSAT) is a four-hour exam comprised of five 35-minute multiple-choice test sections of approximately 25 questions each, plus an essay:

- Reading Comprehension (1 section)
- Analytical Reasoning (1 section)
- Logical Reasoning (2 sections)
- Experimental Section (1 section)

Scoring

- Four of the five multiple-choice sections count toward your final LSAT score
- The fifth multiple-choice section is an experimental section used solely to test new questions for future exams
- Correct responses count equally and no points are deducted for incorrect or blank responses
- Test takers get a final, scaled score between 120 and 180
- The essay is not scored, and is rarely used to evaluate your candidacy by admissions officers

Test Dates

The LSAT is offered four times each year—in February, June, October, and December.

Registration

To register for the LSAT, visit www.LSAC.org to order a registration book or to register online.

GMAT

Structure and Format

The Graduate Management Admission Test (GMAT) is a multiple-choice test for applicants to business school that is taken on computer. It is a computer-adaptive test (CAT), consisting of three sections:

- Two 30-minute essays to be written on the computer: Analysis of an Argument and Analysis of an Issue
- One 75-minute, 37-question Math section: Problem Solving and Data Sufficiency
- One 75-minute, 41-question Verbal section: Sentence Corrections, Critical Reasoning, and Reading Comprehension

The GMAT is a computer-adaptive test, which means that it uses your performance on previous questions to determine which question you will be asked next. The software calculates your score based on the number of questions you answer correctly, the difficulty of the questions you answer, and the number of questions you complete. Questions that appear early in the test impact your score to a greater degree than do those that come toward the end of the exam.

Scoring

You will receive a composite score ranging from 200 to 800 in 10-point increments, in addition to a Verbal score and a Math score, each ranging from 0 to 60. You will also receive an Analytic Writing Assessment (AWA) score ranging from 0 to 6.

Test Dates

The GMAT is offered year-round in testing centers, by appointment.

Registration

To register for the GMAT, call 1-800-GMAT-NOW or register online at www.MBA.com.

Dispelling the Myths about Test Preparation and Admissions

MYTH: If you have a solid GPA, your test score isn't as important for getting into a college or graduate school.

FACT: While it is true that admissions committees consider several factors in their admissions decisions, including test scores, GPA, work or extra-curricular experience, and letters of recommendation, it is not always true that committees will overlook your test scores if you are strong in other areas. Particularly for large programs with many applicants, standardized tests are often the first factor that admissions committees use to evaluate prospective students.

MYTH: Standardized exams test your basic skills or innate ability; therefore your score cannot be significantly improved through studying.

FACT: Nothing could be farther from the truth. You can benefit tremendously from exposure to actual tests and expert insight into the test writers' habits and the most commonly used tricks.

MYTH: There are lots of skills you can learn to help you improve your math score, but you can't really improve your verbal score.

FACT: The single best way to improve your verbal score is to improve your vocabulary. Question types in the verbal reasoning sections of standardized tests all rely upon your understanding of the words in the questions and answer choices. If you know what the words mean, you'll be able to answer the questions quickly and accurately. Improving your critical reading skills is also very important.

MYTH: Standardized exams measure your intelligence.

FACT: While test scores definitely matter, they do NOT test your intelligence. The scores you achieve reflect only how prepared you were to take that particular exam and how good a test taker you are.

Hyperlearning *MCAT Prep Course*

The Princeton Review Difference

Nearly 40% of all MCAT test takers take the exam twice due to inadequate preparation the first time. **Do not be one of them.**

Our Approach to Mastering the MCAT

You will need to conquer both the verbal and the science portions of the MCAT to get your best score. But it might surprise you to learn that the Verbal Reasoning and Writing Sample are the most important sub-sections on the test. That is why we dedicate twice as much class time to these sections as does any other national course! We will help you to develop superlative reading and writing skills so you will be ready to write well crafted, concise essay responses. And of course, we will also help you to develop a thorough understanding of the basic science concepts and problem-solving techniques that you will need to ace the MCAT.

Total Preparation: 41 Class Sessions

With 41 class sessions, our MCAT course ensures that you will be prepared and confident by the time you take the test.

The Most Practice Materials

You will receive more than 3,000 pages of practice materials and 1,300 pages of supplemental materials, and all are yours to keep. Rest assured that our material is always fresh. Each year we write a new set of practice passages to reflect the style and content of the most recent tests. You will also take five full-length practice MCATs under actual testing conditions, so you can build your test-taking stamina and get used to the time constraints.

Specialist Instructors

Your course will be led by a team of between two and five instructors—each an expert in his or her specific subjects. Our instructors are carefully screened and undergo a rigorous national training program. In fact, the quality of our instructors is a major reason students recommend our course to their friends.

Get the Score You Want

We guarantee you will be completely satisfied with your MCAT score!* Our students boast an average MCAT score improvement of ten points.**

*If you attend all class sessions, complete all tests and homework, finish the entire course, take the MCAT at the next administration and do not void your test, and you still are not satisfied with your score, we will work with you again at no additional cost for one of the next two MCAT administrations.

**Independently verified by International Communications Research.

ClassSize-8 Classroom Courses for the GRE, LSAT, and GMAT

Small Classes

We know students learn better in smaller classes. With no more than eight students in a Princeton Review class, your instructor knows who you are, and works closely with you to identify your strengths and weaknesses. You will be as prepared as possible. When it comes to your future, you shouldn't be lost in a crowd of students.

Guaranteed Satisfaction

A prep course is a big investment—in terms of both time and money. At The Princeton Review, your investment will pay off. Our LSAT students improve by an average of 7 points, our GRE students improve by an average of 212 points, and our GMAT students boast an average score improvement of 92.5 points—the best score improvement in the industry.* We guarantee that you will be satisfied with your results. If you're not, we'll work with you again for free.**

Expert Instructors

Princeton Review instructors are energetic and smart— they've all scored in the 95th percentile or higher on standardized tests. Our instructors will make your experience engaging and effective.

Free Extra Help

We want you to get your best possible score on the test. If you need extra help on a particular topic, your instructor is happy to meet with you outside of class to make sure you are comfortable with the material—at no extra charge!

Online Lessons, Tests, and Drills

Princeton Review *ClassSize-8* Courses are the only classroom courses that have online lessons designed to support each class session. You can practice concepts you learn in class, spend some extra time on topics that you find challenging, or prepare for an upcoming class. And you'll have access as soon as you enroll, so
you can get a head start on your test preparation.

The Most Comprehensive, Up-to-Date Materials

Our research and development team studies the tests year-round to stay on top of trends and to make sure you learn what you need to get your best score.

*Independently verified by International Communications Research (ICR).

**Some restrictions apply.

Online *and* LiveOnline *Courses*
for the GRE, LSAT, and GMAT

The Best of Both Worlds

We've combined our high-quality, comprehensive test preparation with a convenient, multimedia format that works around your schedule and your needs.

Online *and* LiveOnline *Courses*

Lively, Engaging Lessons

If you think taking an online course means staring at a screen and struggling to pay attention, think again. Our lessons are engaging and interactive – you'll never just read blocks of text or passively watch video clips. Princeton Review online courses feature animation, audio, interactive lessons, and self-directed navigation.

Customized, Focused Practice

The course software will discover your personal strengths and weaknesses. It will help you to prioritize and focus on the areas that are most important to your success. Of course, you'll have access to dozens of hours' worth of lessons and drills covering all areas of the test, so you can practice as much or as little as you choose.

Help at your Fingertips

Even though you'll be working on your own, you won't be left to fend for yourself. We're ready to help at any time of the day or night: you can chat online with a live Coach, check our Frequently Asked Questions database, or talk to other students in our discussion groups.

LiveOnline *Course*

Extra Features

In addition to self-directed online lessons, practice tests, drills, and more, you'll participate in five live class sessions and three extra help sessions given in real time over the Internet. You'll get the live interaction of a classroom course from the comfort of your own home.

ExpressOnline *Course*

The Best in Quick Prep

If your test is less than a month away, or you just want an introduction to our legendary strategies, this mini-course may be the right choice for you. Our multimedia lessons will walk you through basic test-taking strategies to give you the edge you need on test day.

1-2-1 *Private Tutoring*

The Ultimate in Personalized Attention

If you're too busy for a classroom course, prefer learning at your kitchen table, or simply want your instructor's undivided attention,
1-2-1 Private Tutoring may be for you.

Focused on You

In larger classrooms, there is always one student who monopolizes the instructor's attention. With *1-2-1* Private Tutoring, that student is you. Your instructor will tailor the course to your needs – greater focus on the subjects that cause you trouble, and less focus on the subjects that you're comfortable with. You can get all the instruction you need in less time than you would spend in a class.

Expert Tutors

Our outstanding tutoring staff is comprised of specially selected, rigorously trained instructors who have performed exceptionally in the classroom. They have scored in the top percentiles on standardized tests and received the highest student evaluations.

Schedules to Meet Your Needs

We know you are busy, and preparing for the test is perhaps the last thing you want to do in your "spare" time. The Princeton Review
1-2-1 Private Tutoring Program will work around your schedule.

Additional Online Lessons and Resources

The learning continues outside of your tutoring sessions. Within the Online Student Center*, you will have access to math, verbal, AWA, and general strategy lessons to supplement your private instruction. Best of all, they are accessible to you 24 hours a day,
7 days a week.

*Available for LSAT, GRE, and GMAT

www.PrincetonReview.com

The Princeton Review
Admissions Services

At The Princeton Review, we care about your ability to get accepted to the best school for you. But, we all know getting accepting involves much more than just doing well on standardized tests. That's why, in addition to our test preparation services, we also offer free admissions services to students looking to enter college or graduate school. You can find these services on our website, *www.PrincetonReview.com*, the best online resource for researching, applying to, and learning how to pay for the right school for you.

No matter what type of program you're applying to—undergraduate, graduate, law, business, or medical—**PrincetonReview.com has the free tools, services, and advice you need to navigate the admissions process.** Read on to learn more about the services we offer.

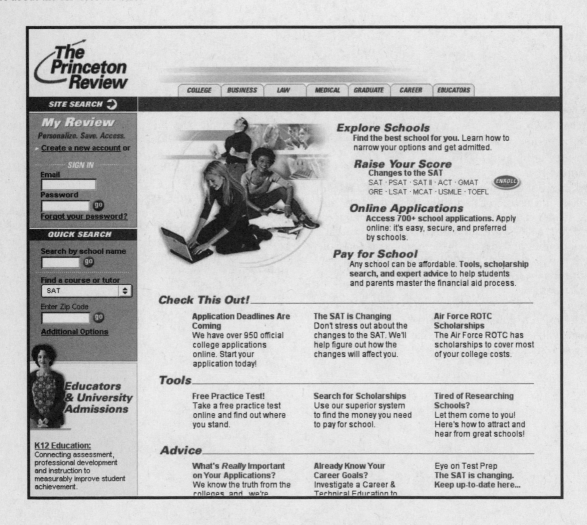

Research Schools
www.PrincetonReview.com/Research

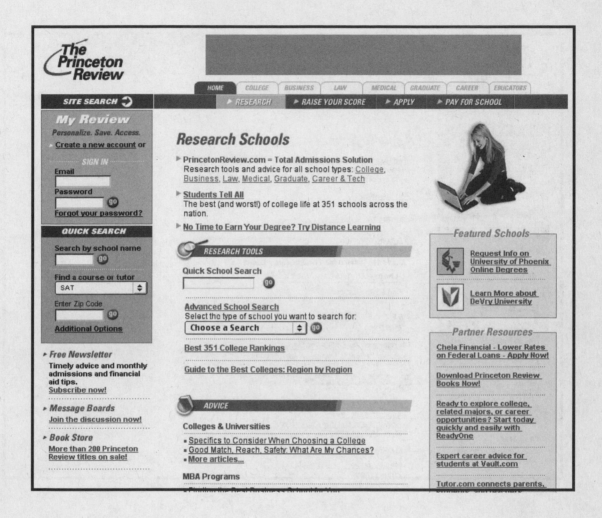

PrincetonReview.com features an interactive tool called **Advanced School Search.** When you use this tool, you enter stats and information about yourself to find a list of schools that fit your needs. From there you can read statistical and editorial information about every accredited business school, law school, medical school, and graduate school.

If you are applying to business school, make sure to use **School Match**. You tell us your scores, interests, and preferences and Princeton Review partner schools will contact you.

No matter what type of school or specialized program you are considering, **PrincetonReview.com has free articles and advice, in addition to our tools, to help you make the right choice.**

Apply to School
www.PrincetonReview.com/Apply

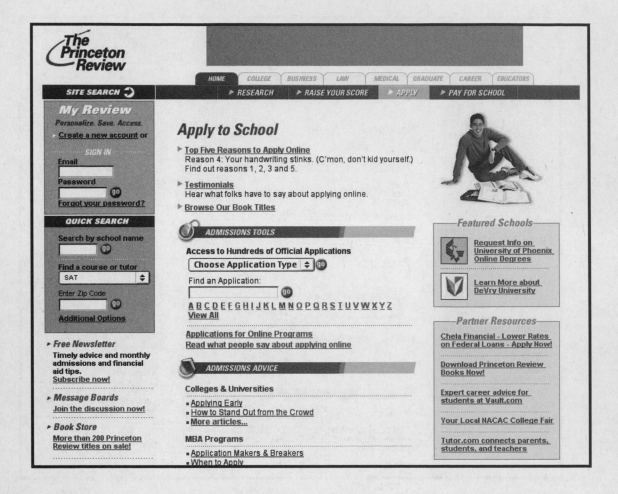

For most students, completing the school application is the most stressful part of the admissions process. PrincetonReview.com's powerful **Online School Application Engine** makes it easy to apply.

Paper applications are mostly a thing of the past. And, our hundreds of partner schools tell us they prefer to receive your applications online.

Using our online application service is simple:

- Enter information once and the common data automatically transfers onto each application.
- Save your applications and access them at any time to edit and perfect.
- Submit electronically or print and mail in.
- Pay your application fee online, using an e-check, or mail the school a check.

Our powerful application engine is built to accommodate all your needs.

Pay for School
www.PrincetonReview.com/Finance

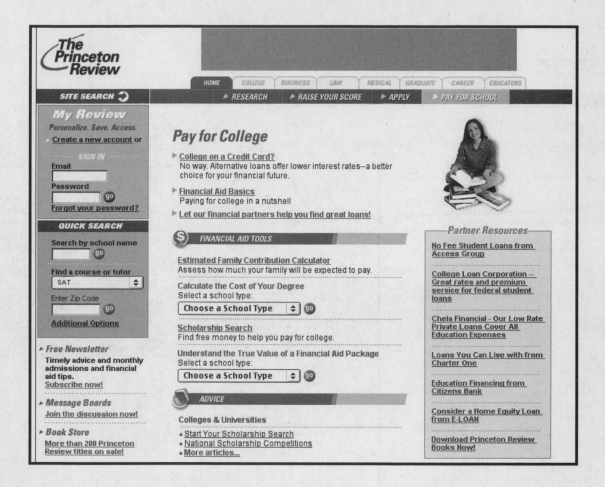

The financial aid process is confusing for everyone. But don't worry. Our free online tools, services, and advice can help you plan for the future and get the money you need to pay for school.

Our **Scholarship Search** engine will help you find free money, although often scholarships alone won't cover the cost of high tuitions. So, we offer other tools and resources to help you navigate the entire process.

Filling out the FAFSA and CSS Profile can be a daunting process, use our **Strategies for both forms** to make sure you answer the questions correctly the first time.

If scholarships and government aid aren't enough to swing the cost of tuition, we'll help you secure student loans. The Princeton Review has partnered with a select group of reputable financial institutions who will help **explore all your loans options**.

If you know how to work the financial aid process, you'll learn you don't have to **eliminate a school based on tuition.**

Be a Part of the PrincetonReview.com Community

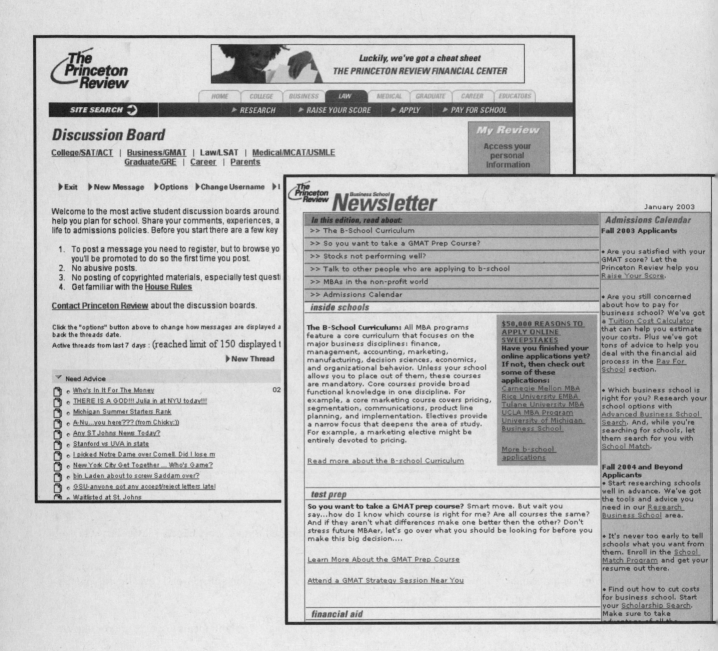

PrincetonReview.com's **Discussion Boards** and **Free Newsletters** are additional services to help you to get information about the admissions process from your peers and from The Princeton Review experts.

Bookstore
www.PrincetonReview.com/college/Bookstore.asp

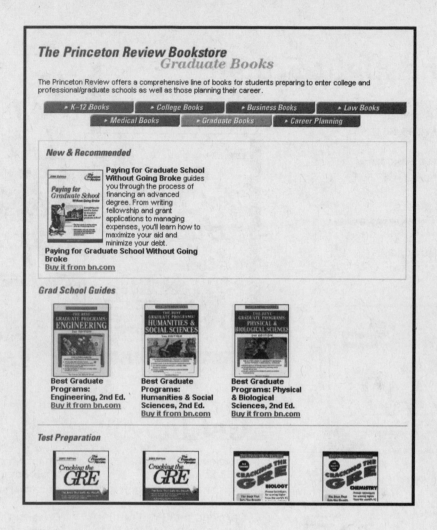

In addition to this book, we publish hundreds of other titles, including guidebooks that highlight life on campus, student opinion, and all the statistical data that you need to know about any school you are considering. Just a few of the titles that we offer are:

- The Best 143 Business Schools
- The Best 117 Law Schools
- The Best 162 Medical Schools
- The Best 357 Colleges
- Complete Book of Graduate Programs in the Arts and Sciences

For a complete listing of all of our titles, visit our **online bookstore**:

www.princetonreview.com/college/bookstore.asp